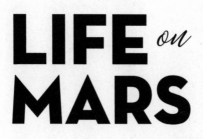

LIFE *on* MARS

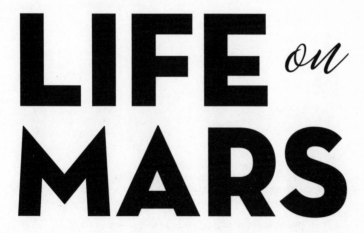

JENNIFER BROWN

BLOOMSBURY

NEW YORK   LONDON   NEW DELHI   SYDNEY

First published in the United States of America in August 2014
by Bloomsbury Children's Books
www.bloomsbury.com

Bloomsbury is a registered trademark of Bloomsbury Publishing Plc

For information about permission to reproduce selections from this book, write to
Permissions, Bloomsbury Children's Books, 1385 Broadway, New York, New York 10018
Bloomsbury books may be purchased for business or promotional use. For information on bulk purchases
please contact Macmillan Corporate and Premium Sales Department at specialmarkets@macmillan.com

Library of Congress Cataloging-in-Publication Data
Brown, Jennifer.
Life on Mars / by Jennifer Brown.
pages   cm
Summary: Twelve-year-old Arcturus Betelgeuse Chambers's quest to find life on other planets seems at an
end when his parents decide to move to Las Vegas, but while they look for a house he stays with his
neighbor, an astronaut who soon becomes a friend.
ISBN 978-1-61963-252-3 (hardcover) • ISBN 978-1-61963-253-0 (e-book)
[1. Astronomy—Fiction.   2. Extraterrestrial beings—Fiction.   3. Astronauts—Fiction.
4. Friendship—Fiction.   5. Family life—Fiction.   6. Moving, Household—Fiction.]   I. Title.
PZ7.B814224Lif 2014   [Fic]—dc23   2013038537

Book design by Nicole Gastonguay
Typeset by Westchester Book Composition
Printed and bound in the U.S.A. by Thomson-Shore Inc., Dexter, Michigan
2 4 6 8 10 9 7 5 3 1

For Scott

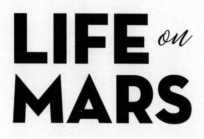

THE BOOGER GALAXY

You would think that my earliest space-related memory would be about, well, space. It would make sense that I'd remember sitting outside, my legs and arms all covered with bug spray, as I wished on shooting stars and peered at the moon through a telescope. Or that I'd recall my father standing next to me, showing me the Big Dipper, the Little Dipper, the North Star.

But, no. My first space-related memory is about boogers. Because that's what happens when you let sisters get involved in things—your best memories get all boogered up.

I was four, and we were lying in the backyard looking for Orion, the Great Hunter in the sky. It was winter, so Dad had pulled our sleeping bags out of the garage and Mom made us hot cocoa, and we were all staring at three stars in a line that Dad said were supposed to make up Orion's belt.

Dad pointed straight up. "You see that haze on his hip, Arty?"

"Yeah," I whispered, goose bumps breaking out on my arms even though the cocoa was making my hands sweat inside my gloves.

"You see it?"

"Yeah, yeah."

"That, Arty, is the Horsehead Nebula."

"The Horsehead Nebula," I repeated, letting out a long, satisfied sigh. "What is it?"

"I just told you. The Horsehead Nebula."

"The Horsehead Nebula," I said again. "What is a nebula made of?"

But before my dad—who knows everything there is to know about the winter sky, the summer sky, and every sky in between—could open his mouth, my older sister, Vega, piped up.

"Boogers," she said, and then giggled. "The whole sky is made of boogers."

Generally speaking, boogers are pretty awesome when you're four. So a nebula made of boogers was a fairly fascinating concept to me. But at that moment my little sister, Cassi, who was barely two and much easier to get along with than she is now, chose to speak her first full sentence:

"Sky is boogers!"

Mom got upset that she had to write "Sky is boogers" in Cassi's baby journal, so she made us go inside. All except for Dad, who had to stay outside and roll up the sleeping bags by himself.

I never got to find out what the Horsehead Nebula was really made of.

I finally found out in fourth-grade space camp that a nebula is a big cloud of gas. But it turns out big clouds of gas are *hilarious* to fourth-grade boys sleeping over in an echoey space museum, so my moment was ruined. Again.

But boogers or no boogers, I could remember that first night so clearly. Orion. My first constellation.

If you step outside on a winter night, and you face southwest and look up, you will see three stars in a line. Those stars are Mintaka, Alnilam, and Alnitak but are more commonly known as Orion's belt. The stars surrounding the belt make up the Orion constellation, a warrior holding a shield in one hand and a club in the other, ready to attack a bull, his sword gleaming in his belt. Muscle, bravery, ferocity! *Ka-pow! Ka-chang! Ka-thud!*

The story goes that Orion was the son of a sea god and a great huntress. It is also said that he got all full of himself and talked smack and a scorpion bit him and he died. And because of that, the Orion constellation and the Scorpio constellation hang out at opposite ends of the sky, so you can never see them at the same time. Orion is pretty much running away from Scorpio every night for all eternity.

So, yeah, he was also kind of a wimp. Because, seriously, a scorpion is just a bug.

Now, if you follow the stars of Orion's belt straight up to the left, you will find a red supergiant. The star that I was named after: Betelgeuse.

Which literally translates to . . . "Armpit."

Okay, "Armpit of the Central One," but to me that only sounded like a really hairy armpit, and kind of sweaty, too, from fighting off bulls and minotaurs and scorpions and stuff.

To be fair, Betelgeuse is only my middle name. My first name is actually Arty, short for Arcturus, which is the alpha star in the Boötes constellation. Being the alpha star sounds pretty important, until you follow it up with Armpit. Armpit kind of makes every name lose its luster. I could've been named after the sun, and if you put Armpit after it . . . again with the sweaty image, am I right?

So, yeah, that's me: Arcturus Betelgeuse Chambers.

There was this famous astronomer named Carl Sagan who figured out all kinds of cool stuff, like that it was trapped gases that made Venus so hot and that there was water on Saturn's moon Titan. And he had this really famous quote that said we are all made of starstuff. What he meant by that was that all of the chemicals that go into our teeth and bones and hair and the food we eat and the cars we drive and the entire planet and pretty much everything came from exploded stars in our universe billions of years ago.

I don't know if I really understand what he was saying. I mean, my third-grade teacher, Mr. Pictor, had the yellowest teeth I'd ever seen on a human being, with little flecks of brown stuck in between the bottom ones. Hard to believe those came from a star. More like from a muddy river, maybe.

But what I do know is that if anyone is made of starstuff,

the Chambers family is definitely it. From Grandpa Muli-phein, who was named after the delta star of Canis Major, to Uncle Fornax, who slept in a lawn chair on his roof during the summer, to my second cousins, Longie and Lattie (short for Longitude and Latitude), right on down to Corvus Chambers—otherwise known as . . . my dad.

Dad worked at the university observatory, a job he'd had since he was an astronomy and physics grad student. That was where he'd met Mom, who was a "cute little co-ed with glis-tening red curls and blah blah blah"—I never knew how the rest of that sentence went because it was disgusting to hear him talk about it. That's my *mom*!

I pretty much grew up in that observatory. Dad would hold my hand, helping me climb the stairs, saying, "Did you know, Arty, that Saturn's rings were first discovered in the sixteen hundreds by Galileo? And we now know that those rings are made up of ice. And *Saturn* has sixty-two moons. . . ." I'd pretend I was walking the catwalk to a space shuttle with my dog, Comet, at my heels, yipping inside a doggy space hel-met. And we'd get up to the top of the stairs and Dad would throw open the door and there would be the giant telescope. Smooth, gleaming, pointing toward the sky as if it were a rocket ready to take off right through the ceiling. It almost took my breath away.

Dad would pat me between the shoulder blades, pushing me toward the eyepiece. "Go ahead," he'd say. "I've already got her trained on Mars for you."

I'd step up on shaky legs and peer through the eyepiece and at first it would be blurry and kind of black around the edges and I would think I couldn't work it or that it was somehow broken. Or maybe a bat was sitting on top of the telescope and all I was seeing was bat butt—which distracted me because I'd crack up trying to say "bat butt" ten times fast in my head.

Bat butt.

Bat butt.

Bat butt.

Bat butt.

Bat butt.

Bat butt.

Bat butt.

Bat butt.

Bat butt.

Bat butt.

"You know, Arty," Dad would say, "they think if there's life out there somewhere, the best bet would be on Mars. All those crevices you see indicate that there might once have been water on Mars, and if there was once, there could still be. Maybe frozen underground. And anywhere there is water, there's potential for life."

I'd look harder and all at once the red planet would come into focus. I would try to see the life he talked about, hoping to find an ocean, maybe see a green blobby head pop out, get a wave from a friendly alien. Maybe the alien would even be wearing a big foam finger: Mars is #1! Mars is #1!

Dad never came home from the observatory early. He liked to stay late, especially on clear summer nights. There was just too much to see.

Which was why it was so surprising when one night my dad came home from work really early, sat down next to me at the kitchen island, threw away the remote control NASA space shuttle replica that had sat on his desk for as long as I could remember, turned to me, and said, "Sky is boogers."

I was about to remind him that it was impossible for the sky to be boogers, because scientists have pretty much identified exactly what ingredients the earth's atmosphere is made of—nitrogen, oxygen, argon, carbon dioxide—and, as you can see, boogers is definitely not one of them, when Mom walked in.

She kissed Dad on the top of his head. "You're home early."

"They did it, Amy," Dad said.

"What?" I asked.

Mom's eyes went wide. "No."

Dad nodded.

"What?" I asked again.

"They couldn't possibly . . . ," Mom said.

"Couldn't possibly what?" I asked.

"Could and did," Dad answered.

"Did what?" I asked, a little louder this time. Though I had begun to suspect that they were ignoring me.

Mom clapped her hand over her mouth. Dad rubbed the top of his bald head a few times, tugged the little clownish hair tufts over his ears till they stood straight out, then announced, "I need to lie down."

After he left, Mom stood completely still, as if she had totally forgotten I was even in the room.

"What just happened?" I asked.

Mom jumped. Then she recovered, smiled, and bent to dig through one of the lower cabinets.

"Want some cookies?" she asked. "I'm going to make double-chocolate chip."

"Oh, no, Mom's baking, what happened?" Vega had walked into the room, her hand permanently attached to her boyfriend, the Bacteria (real name: Mitchell). The Bacteria was kind of an idiot. I imagined the inside of his head to be filled with nothing but a bunch of one-syllable commands: Walk ➡ House ➡ Girl ➡ Hand ➡ Hold ➡ See ➡ Bro ➡ Wave ➡ Duuude.

Although I have always suspected that Vega began hating things on the day she was born, and had only begun hating things with more intensity when she turned fifteen, it wasn't until after she met the Bacteria that she really, really started hating everything in the world. Except him. Gross.

"Something happened," I said.

"Well, of course something happened," Vega said, rolling her eyes and sneering and doing all the things that made her charming and irresistible to someone like the Bacteria. "Mom's baking. Mom always bakes when something happens." There was a clang as Mom sorted through the cookie sheets.

"Don't worry," I said. "She hasn't gotten out the raisins yet. There's nothing to worry about unless she gets out the—"

Mom stood up, unloading an armful of ingredients o
the counter, blew the hair out of her eyes, and then, in slo
motion, she turned, reached up, and pulled a bag out of the
cabinet next to the stove.

Vega gasped so hard her hand almost parted with the Bacteria's hand. "Oh, no. Raisins," she breathed.

That's how I found out that my dad lost his job.

And, with it, I lost my only connection to life on Mars.

2

BRATTIUS: THE SNARLING SISTER STARS

It'd been three weeks since Dad lost his job and so far Mom had made double-fudge brownies, monster cookies, two pineapple upside-down cakes with extra cherries, at least a thousand chocolate chip cookies, lemon bars, a bunch of pies, and a strawberry-chocolate parfait.

All of them had raisins.

Dad spent most of those three weeks wandering aimlessly through the house, munching on sweets, and pulling his hair so much it permanently stuck straight out. Every time someone mentioned anything astronomical in nature, he would get a crazy, bug-eyed look, yank a hair tuft, and disappear into his bedroom.

The result? So far I'd spent my summer waiting for the sun to go down so I could sit on the eaves outside my bedroom window to squint at Mars through the crummy cardboard Mickey Mouse binoculars that Tripp had borrowed from his little brother Chase. And by "borrowed," I mean Tripp sat on Chase's head and threatened to go nebula on him until he said yes.

I couldn't see Mars through those things. All I saw was a faint reddish blur with Mickey Mouse ears on top of it. A drooling twelve-hundred-pound yeti could have been doing the hula on a Martian beach and I wouldn't have been able to see it.

But CICM was too important to get picky about things like binoculars.

CICM had been my pet project since third-grade space camp, when we did a whole unit about life on other planets. CICM stood for Clandestine Interplanetary Communication Module, and the idea behind it was that if I could flash some sort of signal to Mars, and if I did it every night for long enough, eventually the hula-dancing yeti would get curious enough to flash back.

So basically, after three years of constant, committed work, CICM consisted of an intricate and complex system of . . . well, basically a flashlight and some mirrors. And a magnifying glass, because magnifying glasses are awesome. Especially when Tripp duct-tapes one across his forehead so that it hangs over one eye and we play mutant giant-eyed monster tag.

And after three years of dedication, still no flashing yeti.

So I mostly spent my summer nights perched on the roof, trying to see Mickey Mouse Mars, readjusting mirrors, rhythmically pushing the power button on a flashlight, and, most importantly, trying to come up with a better name than CICM—something that would look cool on a T-shirt.

So far I had:

STAR: Stellar Thinktank About Rabid martians

Except that I wasn't interested only in rabid Martians. Actually, if I had a choice, I preferred nonrabid space creatures. And I was pretty positive that the word "Martians" had to be capitalized, making it STARM, which wasn't, technically, a word at all.

PLANET: People Looking At Neptune Every Thursday

Except I had never looked at Neptune a day in my life, mostly because I didn't know where it was, other than next to Uranus, but I dare you to look for something next to Uranus and keep a straight face. It's very distracting.

MARS: Martians Are Real, Steve

I've never known anyone named Steve.

ASTRONOMY: A Secretive Test Run On . . . uhhh . . . way too long

And then I had this great one—People Ogling Other Planets—but that spelled POOP, and even if I wanted to walk around in a shirt with POOP on it, no way would Mom let me wear it to the dinner table.

So my mission remained CICM.

Tonight the only thing standing between me and CICM was my sister Cassi.

When Cassi was a baby, she was cute. She had little pointy elf ears and a wrinkled forehead and every time I stuck my finger in her hand, she grabbed it and squeezed, and she never got bored, no matter how many times I did it. But somewhere between birth and fourth grade, Cassi discovered three things: lip gloss, a loud cheerleading voice, and "being cool."

"Arty, it's your dish night," Mom said after dinner, before migrating into the living room to watch TV with Dad. I groaned. Mom had made double-layer raisin-fudge mint brownies. There were a thousand bowls in the sink.

I turned my gaze over to Cassi and grinned. Her eyes bugged out. She shook her head.

"No way," she said. "I've got cheerleading practice tonight."

"You've got cheerleading practice every night."

"I'm not doing it. Brielle will be here any minute to pick me up."

"What was that? Sorry, I blanked for a minute. I was remembering how much fun we used to have at space camp together."

"No. Stop it! Vega, tell him to stop it."

Vega's eyes barely flicked up from her cell phone, where she was busy texting the Bacteria. "Whatever."

"You don't have to do the dishes, Cassi," I said. "Cassi-ooo . . ."

"No!" she cried! "Stop it! Don't you dare say it, Arty!"

"Cassi-ooo-peee . . ."

"Cut it out! I don't go by that name anymo—"

". . . peee-ahhh. Cassiopeia! Is that Brielle's mom's car I hear running outside? Don't you think she would love to hear about the time you won the rocket-building contest,

Cassiopeia? I'll just run outside and tell her real quick." I acted like I was going to get up.

Cassi stood abruptly, her ponytail swinging forward over the top of her head and lying across her angry eyebrows like an animal. "Fine. I'll do your stupid dishes," she grumbled.

There was once a time when Cassiopeia had her head in the clouds just as much as I did. We went to space camp together, we memorized the planetarium show together, we named our bikes "Spirit" and "Opportunity" after Mars rovers, and yes, she even helped me get CICM up and running.

But ever since getting on the overly pink and glittery cheer squad (all the members of which, I was sure, were named Brielle), Cassi had been on a mission to swear off anything and everything the Brielle Brigade thought was "uncool." From what I could tell, the list consisted of:

1) Parents
2) Teachers
3) Parents who are also teachers
4) Getting your hair wet
5) Siblings of any age
6) Cartoons that feature superheroes with overly large leg muscles
7) All other cartoons
8) Going to a restroom alone
9) Miscellaneous nerdiness, which, according to Cassi, included, "Math; science; or anything that had to do with stars, planets, space in general,

space monsters, aliens, astronauts, rockets, or
any of those geeky scientists who discovered
stuff nobody cares about."

10) Socks that show

So basically Cassi lived with the constant fear that someone would let it slip in front of the Brielle Brigade that she once believed, like me, that there could be life on Mars. And that she once won an award for creating a cotton-ball-and-plastic-tubing water filtration system as a prototype of what humans might use in a man-made ecosystem when we inhabit Mars. And, worst of all, that someone might discover that she was named after nerdy stars.

And what kind of big brother would I be if I didn't take full advantage of that fear? I hadn't done the dishes, taken out the trash, or picked up one doggy package in the backyard in a year.

Cassi stomped away from the table. "I wonder if Earth makes fun of Mars because Mars has no life," she spat, taking our dishes and slamming them into the sink.

I guessed that was supposed to be an insult because I was trying to communicate with said nonexistent life, but I actually thought it was a kind of clever joke, so I chuckled.

Vega slapped her phone down on the table. It beeped again almost immediately. She rolled her eyes. "Duh, Cassi, it's supposed to be, 'If you were a planet, Earth would make fun of you because you have no life.' "

Cassi was in no mood to be corrected. "Shut up, Vega," she said, turning on the sink and dumping about half the bottle of dish detergent into the running water. "You know, Dad's looking for a new job, and I heard him talking to Mom about us maybe having to move. How are you gonna make drooly kissy lips at Mitchell all the time if we don't live in Liberty anymore? What if we move clear out of Missouri? What then?"

Vega grunted and snatched up her phone. "Whatever, Cassiopeia," she said, and in one swift motion shoved her chair back and whipped her body around to leave, her hair swishing behind her. If hair swishing were an Olympic sport, Vega would take home gold. She could swish her hair so hard it felt like a semi just drove past your face.

"Ha-ha, Cassiopeia," I said, pointing at Cassi. But Vega turned and glared at me. "Shut it, Armpit. If we move, what'll happen to your nerd project?"

"It's a Clandestine Interplanetary Communication Module," I corrected, my voice weak.

Vega considered me for a moment, as if she were going to say something back. But her phone beeped (inside the Bacteria's mind: No ➟ Hear ➟ Back ➟ Girl ➟ Push ➟ Phone ➟ Text), and she squeezed it in her palm. "Whatever," she finally said, and walked out of the room.

"I knew you were going to say that," I called after her, but she ignored me. And it appeared that Cassi was also ignoring me, her back turned on me while she frantically scrubbed the dishes. So I sat at the table and chewed my thumbnail, thinking about . . . stuff.

With Cassi you never could be sure if she was telling the

truth or if she was just being dramatic. But if she was telling the truth about us possibly moving, it was bad news.

I didn't want to move. Liberty wasn't the biggest town in the world, but it was my town. I loved that you could count cows in the fields if you drove the back way to school, and that you could walk to the square for the fall festival and ride the Octopus with friends you hadn't planned to see there. I loved the college up on the hill and knowing as you drove into town and saw the brick building roosting above the city in the middle of campus, it meant you were almost home. I loved my school, and I loved it when you sometimes saw your teachers at the community pool or the grocery store. It didn't happen often, but when it did, they always said hi, because that was the way Liberty worked.

I was about to start seventh grade, which meant I successfully survived sixth grade. That might not sound like a big deal, but trust me—living through a week traversing the same hallways as Ben Green and Will Sanchez is such an accomplishment, I was planning to add it to my resume someday:

Arcturus Betelgeuse Chambers, PhD, MD, JD, SD, PQRSWXYZ

• Harvard, Yale, Princeton, Duke, Massachusetts Institute of Technology, and Clown College
Summa cum laude, 700.0 GPA
Voted Most Likely to Rule the Solar System

- Creator of the Chambers Algorithm
- Discoverer of Great Martian Ocean
- Didn't die by the sixth-grade lockers

Once, a sixth grader named Bobby McDoon claimed to have spotted Ben and Will on an Animal Planet predator show chowing down on an antelope. His claim was later proven to be false, but for those of us who regularly tried to make it in one piece from the first-floor restrooms to the third-floor science hall, the story didn't seem far-fetched at all.

But Ben and Will were moving up to high school. Leaving middle school behind. Which meant my posse and I had just as good a chance as any to rule the school.

Or at least to get something of an upper hand on some of the sixth graders on the Lego Robotics team. Until at least October, anyway.

Not to mention, I had Tripp. And Priya. Moving away from them in seventh grade would be like walking out in the middle of the best movie ever. I would always wonder how it was supposed to end. Plus, Tripp had been borrowing money from me since we were five, and by my tally he owed me $12,366. And I would never get it if I moved away.

And then, of course, there was the little matter of CICM. I'd established the eaves on the roof outside my bedroom as the official headquarters. My house was CICM-HQ, which was still way too many consonants in a row to put on a T-shirt, by the way.

I knew that the eaves weren't the only place to see Mars in

July. But they were the best place. They were *my* place. At night, my neighborhood was still and quiet. The curve where the roof met the siding perfectly matched the curve of my back. All of the street lamps were on the other side of the house. And we had only woods behind us—no neighbors junking up visibility with flickering TVs. The eaves were the *perfect* place.

Since I was in a funk, I went up to my bedroom and opened my closet.

And there it was, right between my Einstein T-shirt and my life-sized Yoda cardboard cutout.

CICM.

I pulled it out, being very careful not to loosen the duct tape that held the mirror system together, and carried it across the room. I sat on my bed and gave it a once-over, just to be sure nothing tragic had happened to it in the closet since last night. Its mirrors were duct-taped together in a triad, sort of like mirrors in a fitting room—the kind where you totally can't pay attention to the stupid khakis your mom is making you try on because you're too busy trying to count how many yous in how many positions you can see.

The mirrors sat on a platform. Fastened to the other end of the platform, about four inches away from the mirrors, was a flashlight, its button end facing out, its light end facing the mirrors, with a magnifying glass strategically taped over its lens. But not just any flashlight; one of those fancy superbright ones they stock with the hard-core camping gear. I bought it with my Christmas money.

Everything seemed secure, so I dragged CICM through the window and out onto the eaves. I positioned it in just the right spot, then sat back and got ready for another night of attempting to make history, and of thinking of a better name for CICM.

(Kid Identifying the Solar System? Nope, there was no way I was sitting next to any girl in class with KISS on my shirt. Or worse, sitting next to Tripp with KISS on my shirt.)

At first I sat next to CICM and just looked up at the stars. Draco and Hercules were visible. And low on the horizon, barely visible from my vantage point, was Scorpius, the scorpion that continues to chase Orion menacingly around the sky. (Seriously, Orion, just get a shoe or a rolled-up newspaper or something and smack that sucker!)

After a few minutes of stargazing, I leaned forward, my thumb poised over the flashlight's rubbery button, bending to make sure that the light was pointing toward the mirrors. My left hand hovered near the binoculars hanging around my neck. Maybe tonight would be the night. Tonight I would get a return flash from the red planet. Tonight I would—

A movement caught my eye.

Not from above but from the shadows below.

At first I thought maybe Dad had let Comet out to do his "after-dinner business," which was never good for me, because even though I was the human who fed him and gave him water every day of his life, Comet still barked at me like I was a burglar every time he caught me in CICM-HQ.

But I didn't hear any barking.

Because it wasn't Comet moving around down there. And, trust me, you couldn't miss a dog like Comet. He was big and slobbery and brownish-yellow with droopy eyes and floppy ears and a tail that could double as a weapon when he got really excited—the kind of dog that could regularly eat nonfood things like Tupperware and deck screws and never get sick.

Slowly, I leaned forward and squinted. A man dressed in a pair of black pants and a black hoodie was slinking between our house and the house next door, carrying a trash bag in one fist and a box under the other arm.

I held my breath, freezing with my back up against the side of the house. Holy asteroid, a burglar!

Kind of ironic that now that there was an actual burglar down there wandering around just waiting to be barked at, Comet was nowhere to be found.

I watched as the dark figure picked his way past the trash cans pushed against the side of the house and began trekking toward the woods that went on forever behind our homes. He must have had some elaborate getaway plan involving swinging vines and tunnels and a helicopter with a rescue line.

But just as the figure made it almost to the tree line, my foot involuntarily jerked forward and knocked into the flashlight, dislodging the magnifying glass from its tape and sending it thunking down the eaves. It landed with a clatter on the porch below.

I winced and tried to push myself tighter against the wall

of the house as the man froze in place. Maybe he wouldn't notice. Maybe he wouldn't notice. Maybe he . . . who was I kidding? Of course he was going to notice.

He turned and looked up at me. That's when I caught a glimpse of his face and nearly passed out. His eyes were sunken. He glared. And scowled. Scowled and glared, with a hint of murderous evil eye.

I held my breath.

I couldn't move. My heart was beating in my throat and my knees were knocking together. I was certain that this was going to be the last time I ever looked at Mars, mostly because dead people didn't tend to do a whole lot of anything. I couldn't seem to rip my gaze away from the creepy dark figure even though he was hands-down the scariest thing I'd ever seen in my whole life (and that included the time I walked in on Vega putting some sort of hair-removing foam on her upper lip).

And then he turned, pulled his hood farther up on his head, and disappeared into the woods.

It was as if he'd never been there at all.

But I knew he had.

Because I could scrub my eyeballs with Cassi's super scratchy loofah a thousand times, and I'd still never get that terrifying face out of my head.

3

THE FACE-EATING ZOMBIE CONSTELLATION

The next day, I answered the door to find Tripp crouched on my front porch rubbing his shin. I couldn't count how many times I'd found Tripp this way—grimacing, massaging a knot on his head or sucking on a jammed finger or hopping around on one foot.

Tripp had a real name. It's just nobody could remember it anymore. It may have been Roberto. Or maybe I just imagined it being Roberto because Tripp had freckles and red hair and he didn't look anything at all like a Roberto, so thinking of him as a Roberto was kind of funny.

Actually, it may have been Jason.

Or Todd.

Once I asked his little brother Dodge what Tripp's real name was and even he couldn't remember. Come to think of it, he couldn't remember what his real name was, either. But he did agree that thinking of Tripp as Roberto was funny.

It didn't matter what Tripp's real name was, anyway. Everyone called him Tripp. As in:

Tripped over the teacher's desk on the first day of kindergarten and made her spill her coffee down the front of her dress.

Tripped and fell into the pond surrounding Monkey Island at the zoo on our first-grade field trip, causing the zookeepers to have to shut down Monkey Island for two hours so they could calm down the freaked-out monkeys. Which actually kind of made him a rock star for all of first grade.

Tripped on the first day of middle school and landed on a ketchup bottle, which squirted right into Amber Graham's hair. He was officially no longer a rock star after that.

Tripped and broke his wrist/thumb/ankle/tooth/collarbone/sliding glass door/aquarium/Grandma's prized china plate collection.

Tripp and I had been part of a best friend trio with Priya since preschool, when he fell into me and knocked me face-first into the sandpit. You would think being best friends with such a klutz would be embarrassing, but actually it wasn't. I managed to look really graceful and cool while I was around Tripp. Like a gazelle leaping through the forest. Except that I'd found that comparing yourself to a gazelle leaping through things made people look at you funny and say that you're weird, so I tried not to do it too often.

"I hit that thing," he said when I opened the door. He pointed toward a moving van at the house that separated his house from mine. The house had been empty for months, ever since the Feldmans moved out. "I didn't see it and I walked right into it," Tripp finished. He stood, tested out some weight on his foot by bouncing up and down a little.

"You didn't see that giant moving van," I repeated.

He shook his head. "Sprung right up on me."

I believed it. I'd seen surprising things spring up on Tripp many times before. Whole walls, for example.

He bounced a few more times, then smiled. "I'm good," he said. "Do I smell cookies?" He pushed past me and walked into the house, following his nose toward the kitchen. "So who's moving in? Hope he's our age and has a motorcycle."

The last thing on earth Tripp needed was a motorcycle.

We rounded the corner into the kitchen, where Mom was sliding warm oatmeal cookies off a cookie sheet onto a cooling rack. Tripp made a beeline for them, stumbling over a stool leg and almost taking the entire cooling rack to the floor with him but catching himself just in time.

"Hello, Tripp," Mom said, completely unfazed. Mom was used to Tripp, too. I suppose once you see a kid take out the entire handrail on your basement steps, almost losing a few cookies seems like no big deal.

"Hey, Other Mom," Tripp answered, cramming a cookie into his mouth.

"We've got new neighbors," I said, picking up a cookie and sniffing it, then putting it back onto the cooling rack. "Have you met them?"

Mom shook her head. "No, but I think it's just one man. Nobody your age." She plopped more dough onto the cookie sheet in little mounds. If she didn't stop, we were all going to turn into raisins. We would have to change our name to the Raisin Family. I would have to wear raisin pants, and every time I opened my mouth to talk, a raisin would fly out, and I'd just keep growing raisin-ier and raisin-ier until eventually I turned into a giant raisin monster and then Tripp would have to come after me, shooting an oatmeal cookie batter cannon at me from his motorcycle until I—growling, of course, because all giant monsters made of food growl—exploded and rained down tiny bits of raisins on the whole city.

Actually, that sounded kind of awesome. I picked up the cookie again and ate it in two bites.

"Does the new guy drive a motorcycle?" Tripp asked.

"I didn't see one," Mom said. "I think he's a bit older."

"Aw, man," Tripp said, "just some boring old guy, then."

"How do you know he's boring? You haven't even met him yet," Mom said.

Tripp's eyes lit up. "Yeah, you're right. He could be mean and scary with gnarled-up fingernails and acid breath, and he could sleep in a coffin. That would be so cool!"

"Well, now you're making him sound like a vampire, Tripp," Mom said.

Immediately I thought about the guy I'd seen the night before. "Mom," I said, "have you seen him? What does he look like?"

She shook her head. "I haven't. I think your dad has. You can ask him later."

I didn't need to ask Dad. Deep in my gut, I already knew. The burglar in the hoodie I'd seen last night . . . was moving in!

I grabbed Tripp's sleeve and pulled. "Come on, let's go," I said.

"Bot om ayting," he said around a mouthful of cookie.

"You can eat it and walk at the same time." I actually had my doubts about that. Tripp could do almost nothing and walk at the same time.

"Where we going?" he asked when we got outside on the sidewalk.

"To Priya's," I told him.

If you live in North America, you can see a V-shaped constellation in the fall night sky. It's Andromeda, the Chained Maiden. Andromeda's dad was King Cepheus and her mom was Cassiopeia, who supposedly ticked off the sea nymphs by getting all braggy that she was so much more beautiful than they were. So the sea nymphs tattled on her to Poseidon, who got upset, and, trust me, Poseidon is not a dude you want to get mad at you. Next thing you know, Poseidon was sending some monster to destroy Cepheus's land. Basically the only way Cepheus and Cassiopeia could get out of it was to sacrifice their beautiful daughter, Andromeda, to the sea monster.

So they totally did. I know, parents of the year, right? Why couldn't they have been the ones bitten by the scorpion?

Anyway, so they chained Andromeda to a rock and she would have been sea monster supper had Perseus not come along and seen how amazingly stunning and soft she was and fallen in love. Long story short, Perseus saved Andromeda and they got married.

Sometimes, when I thought about that story, and about the beautiful and gentle Andromeda, I thought of Priya.

And that was a new thing, believe me. And, no, I didn't know where it came from, either.

But I couldn't help it. Priya started wearing these bracelets that clinked and clanked on her arm, and sometimes she bit her lip when she was thinking hard about an algebra problem, and all of it was very . . . Andromeda-like.

But if you tell Tripp I said that, I'll kill you.

Priya lived across the street and two houses down, and her mom and my mom were best friends. Priya was also in our preschool class. She was the one who picked me up out of the sandpit and wiped the sand off the front of my shirt. And then she helped Tripp get up. And then she let us both share her juice box so we could get the sand out of our mouths.

Tripp was so into licking the cookie crumbs off his fingers, he forgot to look up and stubbed his toe on Priya's front porch step, pitching him forward into the door. So instead of knocking like normal people, we knocked like *ka-thud boom!* But Priya was every bit as used to opening her front door to a just-tripped Tripp as I was, so she didn't notice.

"What's up?" she asked. She was holding a marker and had a smudge of orange across the bridge of her nose.

I pointed to the moving van. "We got new neighbors," I said.

"So?"

"So, I have to tell you guys something. Come on."

They didn't ask, just followed me across the street and back down to my house, where we went up to CICM-HQ (minus CICM, since it was technically broken and Comet had probably peed on the magnifying glass by now, because Comet peed on everything unusual he found in the backyard).

I told them all about what I'd seen the night before—the old man in the black hoodie. The bag of body parts he was carrying. The box of more body parts or perhaps implements of torture of seventh-grade children. The way he scowled at me from beneath his hood, his eyes all shadowy like a vampire's.

"So you think he's a vampire," Priya said disbelievingly.

"No." (Maybe.)

"A monster?"

"Definitely not." (Definitely maybe.)

She rolled her eyes. "So you think he's a . . . what? Serial killer?"

I forced out a laugh. (Yes. Yes, yes, absolutely, definitely, without a doubt yes.) "No."

"I know what he is," Tripp said. "He's a zombie. The undead. And inside that box was a shovel for him to dig himself out of his grave. And the bag was full of human faces."

"Exactly," I said, because sometimes my mouth moves before my brain can catch up.

"One, that's disgusting," Priya said, holding up a finger. You never wanted to argue with Priya when she started listing points in one-two-threes, because usually by the time she got to four, your argument was cooked. She held up a second finger. "Two, why would he need to carry around the shovel when he's already outside of the grave?"

"To pull the dirt back in on himself when he's done eating the faces. Duh," Tripp said.

"And three, zombies don't eat faces, they eat brains."

"How do you know?" Tripp challenged. "You've never even seen a zombie."

"And you have?" Priya asked.

"Yeah, in like a hundred movies and stuff."

I slapped my hand over my forehead. You always knew Tripp was going to lose an argument when he started adding "and stuff" to the end of his sentences.

"Seriously, Tripp, you watch way too much TV." She turned to me. "But you can't possibly really believe he's a zombie."

"All I know is he was very creepy. I'm pretty sure he's related to the Grim Reaper. His name is probably Mr. Death. And he wasn't just holding the box and bag, he was *taking* them somewhere. Out there." I pointed toward the tree line. Priya's forehead scrunched up as she considered it.

"Maybe it was just trash and he was littering," she said. "He is moving in, after all. When my aunt moved, she had tons of trash."

"Still a criminal," Tripp said triumphantly. "Just like I was saying."

Priya held up a finger. "One, a litterbug is not exactly the same kind of criminal as a murderer. And two, you weren't saying he was a criminal, you were saying he's a zombie."

"I'm pretty sure it's illegal to eat people's faces, Priya," Tripp said.

"Brains! Brains, not faces!"

They continued to argue, but I tuned them out, concentrating instead on Mr. Death's house. I saw movement behind the curtains in one of the back rooms. I knew that room from going in and helping Widow Feldman move a TV once. Mrs. Feldman had always hung sheer white curtains back there, and when the weather was nice she'd open the window and you could see the curtain fluttering in the breeze. But now the window was covered with heavy curtains, and they were pulled together tightly.

But there was definitely movement behind them.

"You guys," I whispered. But they didn't stop arguing, so I said it louder. "You guys! Look!"

They both stopped, and all of our eyes were glued to the curtains as they went from slight fluttering to more notable rippling.

"Do you think he's watching us?" Priya asked.

"What are you scared of, Priya, if he's not a zombie?" Tripp asked, but you could hear it in his voice—he was totally scared, too.

"Shut up, Tripp," I said. I squinted harder. Harder. Harder. And then suddenly the curtain was yanked back completely, and Mr. Death's pale face and penetrating eyes were staring right out at us.

We all screamed and grabbed at one another, then scrambled back through my bedroom window.

Well, Priya and I scrambled. Tripp . . . tripped.

4

THE BLACK HOLE OF LAS VEGAS

One night, a few weeks later, I was up in CICM alone. I'd come up with an idea about refracting the light off a closer mirror in order to get a brighter flash, and I wanted to try it out. I strapped a couple of old compact mirrors that Mom donated to CICM onto the sides of the flashlight and clicked the button a couple of times. I couldn't tell for sure, but it looked like the beam got brighter.

And that's when I heard noise coming from around the side of the house again. Quickly, I snapped off the light and shimmied backward. Now that Mr. Death definitely knew about CICM, I was afraid that he'd use his superhuman zombie climbing powers to scale the side of my house and eat my face off before I could even cry for help.

Not really.

Okay, yeah, really.

The point was, I didn't want to get caught.

I held my breath and prayed that he couldn't hear my heart-beat. I watched until my vision got grainy and I wasn't sure if he was moving or if I was just seeing things. There were more noises and maybe a meaty smell, but I couldn't be sure, and then just as he rounded the corner and our eyes met . . .

"Arty!"

It was Cassi and her constant companion: her giant mouth.

"Ar-teee!" My bedroom light flipped on, bathing the back-yard in light. "I know you're out there, you creeper. You need to come downstairs. Now! Family meeting! Dad said!"

I glanced back at Mr. Death just as he turned and walked into the woods.

"Arty!" she shouted again. "I know you hear me!"

I swiveled in through the window, yanked it shut, and dropped to my hands and knees. "Shhh! Do you want to get us both killed?" I crawled over to the light switch, reaching up only enough to paw it off.

"You. Are. So. Embarrassing," Cassi said, then turned and tromped downstairs.

Once upon a time, we had family meetings often. Mom said it would make us all closer so that when we were grown up and they weren't around anymore, my sisters and I would still have each other's backs. We'd had dozens of family meetings, and while I didn't feel any closer to Vega or Cassi, I did like the board games we sometimes played.

We hadn't had a family meeting at all since Dad lost his job.

So why were we having one now?

Suddenly, I was more worried about what awaited me in the family den than about Mr. Death wandering around outside looking for a place to bury his dead bodies or eat faces. Slowly, I crept downstairs.

Dad was sitting in his recliner; his hair tufts, for once, were flat against his head. Vega was parked on the sofa, with her hand glued to the Bacteria. Cassi was sitting cross-legged on the floor next to Comet, doing some sort of cheerleader stretch. Mom placed a plate of still-steaming banana nut bread on the coffee table. The Bacteria immediately leaned forward and swiped a piece.

Warily, I kneeled next to the table.

"What's going on?" I asked.

"Family meeting," Mom said brightly, perching on the arm of Dad's chair.

"But why are we—?"

"No raisins," Vega interrupted, pointing at the last crumb of bread in the Bacteria's hand. She whipped around to Mom. "You didn't put raisins in this bread."

Mom shrugged. "I got tired of them."

Vega and I exchanged glances. Dad's tufts were combed down and Mom was tired of raisins?

She gasped. "You got a job!"

Dad smiled. "Well, I was hoping to be the one to break the news, but . . . yes, I did."

Cassi squealed and clapped her hands. I let out a cheer. Vega's eye roll was a little less rolly than usual (which, trust me, is as close to cheering as Vega comes). Even the Bacteria let out a whoop (a one-syllable whoop, of course).

"Congratulations, Daddy," Cassi said. "Can I get a phone?"

"Well, before you . . . ," Dad began.

"No way you're getting a phone. I had to wait until sixth grade to get one," Vega shot to Cassi, overriding Dad.

"So what? You weren't in cheer. I need a phone. Mom said . . ."

Dad tried again. "Listen, before anyone gets anything . . ."

"What? Mom!" Vega yelled. "You can't get her a phone. I was, like, the last person in the entire middle school to get one, and it was so humiliating, and you said . . ."

"Nobody's getting a phone," Mom said, holding her hands out toward my sisters like she was directing traffic.

Cassi yelped. "You said I could get one. Not fair! It's none of Vega's—"

"It's totally fair. Armpit should get one before you do, and he doesn't even have one yet," Vega yelled.

Technically, she had a point. I should have gotten a phone before Cassi, just by sheer seniority. However, I had no desire for a phone, so it didn't really matter to me if Cassi got one or not.

"No way! If I have to wait for Armpit, I'll never get one. He has, like, zero friends to call anyway."

Whoa. Not true. What were Tripp and Priya—chopped liver? Also? My name is not Armpit. Just reminding everyone.

"Now, Cassiopeia," Mom said, which got Cassi bellowing.

"You called me that name again! I can't believe after you said you would stop calling me that . . ."

And Vega started yelling at the Bacteria about how horrible her life was in fifth grade without a phone, and the Bacteria nodded with big eyes and just kept saying, "Totes," his one-syllable way of saying "totally." And Mom was apologizing, which was doing no good because when Cassi started really wailing, Comet began howling right along with her, the same way he sometimes did when a fire truck drove down the street.

And me? I watched, wishing I had some popcorn for this special family bonding moment and considered running into the kitchen real quick to pop a bag.

Until right in the middle of it all, Dad gave his hair tufts one mighty yank with both fists and yelled out, *We're moving! The job is in Las Vegas!*

And just like that, everyone fell totally silent.

5

THE BIG SCREAM THEORY

Vega was the first, but definitely not the loudest, to freak out.

It went like this: Shouting, shouting, shouting about cell phones and stuff. Then Dad hollering that we were moving to Vegas. Then total silence, during which time Comet figured it would be a good idea to stop howling and instead loudly lick his foot. And we all looked at each other in slow motion— *tick, tick, tick.* And then . . .

KABOOM! Big Bang number two, the Chambers Family Phenomenon, wherein a giant explosion occurred right in my living room.

"What? *Vegas?* No way! You can't do this to us, Daddy!" Vega cried, and buried her face in the Bacteria's shoulder, bawling her eyes out.

And at almost exactly the same moment, Cassi started screaming so loudly that Comet stopped midlick and threw back his head and howled some more. "But what about cheerleading? Mom, you know how important this is to me. You know how hard I've worked."

And the Bacteria kept repeating "Dude" over and over again while kind of awkwardly petting the back of Vega's head, his other hand inching forward—reaching, *reaching* for the banana bread. Girl ➡ Cry ➡ Dude ➡ Bread ➡ Yum.

And Mom started shouting at Cassi. And Dad started shouting at nobody. And our living room sounded like this:

"I WON'T GO YOU CAN'T MAKE ME BUT IT'S MY JOB AND YOU'LL LOVE VEGAS YOU'VE GOT THE SAME NAME BUT WHAT ABOUT MITCHELL *HOOOOOOWL* CHEERLEADING AND BRIELLE AND NOW I'LL BE A SOCIAL OUTCAST AND CASSI THEY HAVE CHEERLEADING IN VEGAS AND MITCHELL MITCHELL MITCHELL *HOOOOOOWL* NOW LOOK WE HAVE TO PULL TOGETHER AS A FAMILY WE'RE IN LOVE YOU CAN'T DO THIS TO US CHEER IS MY LIFE I WILL NEVER FORGIVE YOU *HOOOOOOWL* DUDE THIS BREAD IS SO GOOD OH MY GOSH ARE YOU EATING BREAD OUR LIVES ARE OVER AND YOU'RE EATING BREAD DUDE NO DUDE *HOOOOOWL* I HATE YOU I HATE EVERYONE I HATE LIFE *HOOOOOWL* BUT DUDE BREAD."

Then Dad stood up, raised both of his hands, and hollered so loud that Comet ran into the kitchen and disappeared out through his doggy door.

"That's enough! We are moving and that is that!"

"But . . . Mitchell," Vega started, big smudgy makeup marks all over her face, which, from the looks of things, fairly disgusted the Bacteria, whose crumb-covered mouth was drawn down in a grimace.

Dad pointed at her. "No. Not a word."

"But this is so unfair," Cassi cried from across the room, her hands planted on her hips and her whole face puckered into a pout.

Dad pointed at her. "Zip it."

"Well, I hope you're happy," Cassi said, stomping out of the room. "You've ruined my life. It's over. I might as well just . . . grow horns and join the circus."

"I don't think it's possible to grow horns on purpose. Especially if you're a human," I pointed out, but she just glared at me over her shoulder.

"And I might as well buy an old-maid dress," Vega piped up. "Because I will never love anyone again!"

I was tempted to ask what an old-maid dress looks like but decided against it, given that she had disengaged her hand from the Bacteria's, so I knew this was serious business. Vega covered her face with both of her hands and ran out of the room, her sobs muffled and snotty sounding in her palms.

"Vega!" Mom said, and rushed out after her. Dad, the Bacteria, and I took turns picking at things—the carpet, a napkin, a hair tuft—and pretending that none of that had just happened.

Finally, Dad cleared his throat. "Well, I suppose that didn't go exactly as I planned," he said.

"Dude, whoa." The Bacteria stood up. "I should go."

"Yes, that would probably be wise. From the sound of things, Vega isn't going to be very good company for tonight."

"Yeah," the Bacteria said, edging around the coffee table. "Bye." He started toward the door, then at the last minute, darted back, snatched up the last three pieces of banana bread, and took off. "Yum," he said, just before closing the front door behind him.

There's a saying that my Grandpa Muliphein once taught me. It goes, "Still waters run deep." He told me that meant that sometimes people who don't say very much are thinking a whole lot and are very smart, so you shouldn't ever judge a quiet person to be a dumb person.

I'm pretty sure Grandpa Muliphein had never met the Bacteria.

With my sisters locked in their rooms and Mom racing back and forth between them, trying to console them, it was just Dad and me left in the living room. Dad and me and the *hum-whoosh* of the dishwasher in the kitchen.

And there was something about that *hum-whoosh* that made it really sink in what had just gone on. My sisters weren't just being their typical dramatic selves. They had a point. This was sort of a big deal.

We were moving.

Moving.

Away from . . . everything. Away from our *hum-whoosh*ing dishwasher and away from the stop sign on the corner that rattled when the wind blew and away from Comet's peed-on swing-slash-nemesis. Away from Priya and Tripp and Liberty Middle School with its awesome pizza and its baseball diamonds where I played Little League until we all realized that I was much more likely to use a baseball to make a model of the solar system than to actually hit with a bat. Away from the tornado slide at my old elementary school, even though I hadn't slid on it since second grade when Mattie Frankelberger pushed me off the top step to see if I could really fly into space. Away from Mattie Frankelberger. Which, okay, wasn't necessarily a bad thing, even though she now went by Matilde and wore colored stripes in her hair and could play the drums like nobody's business. She still had pushy-looking hands. Away from seventh grade, which was supposed to be my best year yet.

And, especially, away from CICM-HQ and the sparkling Liberty skies.

"Dad?" I asked.

He didn't answer. Just stared straight ahead.

"Dad?" I repeated.

He blinked. "Huh?"

"Isn't it, like . . . really bright in Las Vegas?"

"Vegas," he repeated softly. "You'll love Vegas." Which, obviously, was not an answer to my question.

"I mean, I've seen Vegas in movies and stuff and aren't there a lot of lights?"

"No, they may not have a Mitchell in Vegas, but is that really a bad thing?" He focused on me for a second. "Is it, Arty? Is no Mitchell a bad thing?"

I shrugged. "More banana bread for the rest of us, I guess."

"Exactly!" Dad clapped once. "There will be more banana bread in Vegas! Not exactly sure what that means, but it sounds positive and I'll take all the positive I can get. I mean, it's Vegas. Who wouldn't be excited about moving to Vegas?"

"Cassi, Vega . . . ," I said.

"Yes, but your sisters will come around. They'll see. You get it. This is an adventure, right, Arcturus?"

"Right, but, Dad, I was asking about the lights in Vegas, because as we all know, bright lights can . . ."

He clapped his hands again and hopped on his toes a little bit. "Yes, bright lights! Like Christmas all the time!" He paced a couple steps, then turned and paced back, tugging at his hair tufts with each step. "An adventure! Banana bread! Christmas all year round! I'll just have to convince them."

"No, I wasn't suggesting . . . I was wondering if the lights would make it hard to . . ."

"You are very smart, Arcturus. Very smart indeed. They'll come around. I just have to make them see. This is best for all of us."

Just then, there was the sound of a door slamming upstairs, followed by more wailing—Cassi and Vega together, in two-part harmony.

He snapped his fingers, excitedly, paced past me, patting my shoulder twice as he went by. "Thanks, son," he said.

"You're welcome," I said, then followed him across the

living room. "But, Dad, I was actually a little worried that the lights in Vegas might make it kind of hard to . . ."

He gestured over his shoulder as he hightailed it toward the stairs. "We'll talk more about our Vegas adventure later, Arty," he called, and then disappeared.

". . . see the sky," I finished after he'd gone.

6

THE ROCKET SHIP OF DOOM

When I rang Tripp's doorbell, I heard a tumbling sound from inside the house, and then the door was pulled open to reveal Tripp rubbing his backside with both hands.

"I fell down the stairs," he said, although I noticed him cast an accusing glance over his shoulder toward his older brother, Heave, who stood at the top of the stairs with a wicked grin on his face. Heave shrugged, which is usually the job of Tripp's oldest brother, Shrugg, but at the moment Shrugg was racing through the living room after Chase, wearing only a pair of tightie whities and screaming something about paybacks. Tripp edged through the door and closed the chaos in behind him. "What's up?" he asked.

"Rocket ship," I replied.

Tripp's eyebrows went up. "We haven't been there since Priya's mom made her take swimming lessons in fourth grade," he whispered.

He was right. Otherwise known as the Great Deep End Freakout. We really hadn't been to the rocket ship in ages.

The rocket ship was an ancient play structure on our elementary school playground. It was made out of recycled tractor tires and was so old, Dad once told me that Grandpa Muliphein helped build it when my dad was in elementary school back in the 1980s. Over the years, the school had built a real playground around it, with fancy monkey bars and tunnel systems and, of course, the aforementioned infamous tornado slide. But even though we had all the fancy stuff, the school never got rid of the tire rocket ship, and every spring Dad would go out there with little cans of paint and repaint it, white and gray and blue, with windows that reflected a marbled moon.

Nobody ever played in the rocket ship.

Except Tripp, Priya, and me. We spent more hours than I could count inside those tires, nasally talking into our cupped hands: "*Crrr*, Houston, we have Mars in sight, I repeat, we have Mars in sight, over, *Crrr. Crrr*, ten-four, Bald Eagle, you may land whenever you feel like it, over, *Crrr. Crrr*, that would be now, Houston, I've been in this rocket for six months and I really have to pee, over, *Crrr*."

And then we'd giggle until we really did have to pee. And once Tripp giggled until he actually peed, and he had to go to the nurse's office and wear the nurse's donated office pants, and we just told everyone that he sat on a juice box, because that's what friends do when a giggle-pee happens. You never know when a giggle-pee could happen to you.

But somewhere around fourth grade, the rocket ship

started to get uncool. And also a little small. And a group of kindergartners kept hanging around pretending to be hostile aliens, and we could never land, not even to pee.

But my dad's news the night before was rocket ship–worthy. I'd called Priya before I'd walked to Tripp's house. I'd even talked into my cupped hand over the phone for authenticity. She didn't giggle, so I felt stupid.

"What's going on?" Tripp asked, pulling a bacon-flavored toothpick out of his pants pocket, blowing a ball of lint off it, and stuffing it into his mouth. "Want one? I'm pretty sure I've got another one in here somewhere."

I shook my head. The thought of what he might have to blow off a toothpick found "in there somewhere" made my stomach squish. "I'll tell you when we get there. And I thought your mom banned toothpicks from your house after Dodge sat on one and had to have it taken out in the emergency room with a pair of tweezers."

"She did. I found some loose ones under my dresser this morning. Sure you don't want one? They still have a little flavor left in 'em."

I made a face. "No thanks."

We walked to our old school, just like we'd done a million times, both of us talking about good old elementary school memories, and I wished more than anything that we could go back to that. Back to before middle school, when suddenly everybody was so worried about looking cool and playing sports and back when my dad had his job at the university observatory and it looked like things would stay that way forever. Back to a time when leaving my best friends would have been the last thing on my mind.

Priya was waiting for us when we got there. "Perchlorate," she said.

"Huh?" Tripp asked.

"Perchlorate. It's in the soil on Mars. My dad saw an article about it on the Internet. You know what that means."

We both looked at her, totally blank.

"Life. It means there could have been life there. Which can only mean . . ." She got a very serious look on her face and we leaned forward. "Mars probably has face-eating zombies, too." She threw her head back and laughed. "Boo!" she said, making her hands into claws and lunging toward Tripp.

"Har har har, you're so funny," Tripp said, but he'd jumped just a little. I'd felt it.

"I'm just teasing you, Tripp," she said, bumping his shoulder with hers. "So, why the rocket ship meeting? More about the monster next door?"

"Yeah, what's up with the undead behind Widow Feldman's curtains?" Tripp asked.

"I'm not here to talk about that," I said. "Come on." I knelt down in front of the opening of the rocket ship. It had gotten even smaller since the last time I saw it.

"We have to go in that thing?" Priya asked, scowling. "There are bugs in there."

Tripp and I froze. "Since when do you care about bugs?" Tripp asked. "You used to eat them."

She rolled her eyes at him. "I ate one grasshopper one time, to prove to you that they weren't poisonous."

I leaned into Tripp, grinning. "Oh, that was so gross. Its leg got stuck in the corner of her mouth and it kept wiggling every time she talked and it was all hairy and you puked, remember, Tripp?"

Tripp nodded, then gagged, his face turning red. "See?" he choked out. "You weren't scared of bugs then. You were one of the guys."

"Yeah, you were more of a guy than Tripp," I said, and Tripp slugged my shoulder.

"Fine," Priya said. "Let's just go in."

We ducked into the tires, bent low, picking our way through the slimy puddles that collected in there, year-round. Finally we got to the end, and Priya folded herself up against a tire. I took my position in the oxidizer, and then Tripp came in last, smacking his head on the bottom of the upper tire. He sat, rubbing his forehead the same way he'd been rubbing his rump earlier.

"So? What's the deal?" Priya asked. "Why are we here?"

I looked at my best friends, ready to fly the pretend ship wherever I wanted it to go, and I was suddenly hit with such sadness at leaving them behind, breaking up the trio, I did the only thing I could think to do.

I cupped my hand over my mouth.

"*Crrr*, Houston, we have a problem. I'm moving."

Over.

Crrr.

7

THE WAILING RAINBOW STAR

"Arty, you need to get up," Mom said, waking me from a deep sleep.

"Huh?" I said, lifting my head from beneath the pillow. I think for as long as I live, I will never figure out how my head goes to sleep on top of a pillow every night and wakes up under it every single morning.

"Rise and shine!" Mom whipped open the window blinds in one loud ripping sound. Sunlight streamed in, and I shrank back and growled like a vampire.

Speaking of vampires . . . (Or zombies.)

Ever since I found out we were moving, I was doing as much neighbor watching as I was Mars watching. I almost even considered adding it as official CICM business. Clandestine Interplanetary Communication Mission and Terrifying Zombie Neighbor Observatory. CICMTZNO. At least I finally got another vowel in there.

Every night, Mr. Death would leave his house, always carrying a trash bag in one hand and a box in the other. Always wearing a black hoodie. And always disappearing into the trees. He never came back, no matter how long I waited. I stared into the woods until my eyes were droopy and CICM's batteries were dead from all the flashing and my feet were numb from keeping my legs crossed for so long.

And every night I waited while Comet went out for his nightly ritual, which consisted of first tugging on Cassi's old swing as if he were trying to kill it (because Comet was always trying to kill things that weren't actually alive—like socks and pieces of rope), and then giving up and just peeing on it instead. He'd been peeing on that swing for years. I'd seen him do it probably a thousand times. And I would have told Cassi, but then the Brielle Brigade would come over and call me "Supernerd" or "Spacedork" and I would just—oops!—forget to mention that their sequined, shiny white outfits were sitting on Comet's favorite toilet. Sometimes I would even find Comet and high-five his paw.

Anyway, every night I waited until Comet got his nightly ritual over with and the house shut down and Mom came in and told me good night, and then I would get really scared because all of a sudden it was entirely too quiet for anything good to be going on.

And still Mr. Death would never come back from the woods.

I was beginning to think maybe Tripp had a valid theory

(eleven words I never thought I'd hear myself say). Maybe Mr. Death wasn't coming back because he had reburied himself for the night.

Sometimes Priya's mom and mine would get caught up talking Mom Stuff, and it would get late, and Priya would join me. When that happened, we would call Tripp over, though a few times he wasn't home, which we both found curious. Tripp was always home. And if he wasn't, at least one of us knew where he was. Once, we stayed up at CICM so long, we saw Tripp's dad's car pull into his driveway, and we saw Tripp's silhouette spill out of the car, a duffel slung over one shoulder. Even though we called his name about a hundred times, he scurried in through his garage, like he never heard us at all.

"Did that seem weird to you?" Priya asked.

I shrugged. "What do you expect? Tripp's weird," I said, even though, yeah, I totally thought it was weird. But Priya simply nodded and we went back to our lookout.

"Hey, Priya."

"Huh?"

"What do you think Mr. Death does out there?"

"I don't know. Maybe he meditates or prays or something. Or hunts."

"Hunts people?"

"No, silly. Animals. Maybe he traps rabbits. My cousin knows how to make rabbit traps." But I could see it in the way she bit her lip as she held the Mickey binoculars to her face—even Priya was a little bit frightened.

That was why I growled, vampire-style, when Mom pulled open my blinds. I had been up way too late the night before, wondering exactly what Mr. Death was hunting out there, and if he knew how to make seventh-grade-boy traps, too.

"Come on, you've got to get up," Mom repeated. "Ugh." She made a face as she picked up a used pair of underwear that had been draped over the back of my desk chair and dropped them into my clothes hamper. "You've got to get yourself presentable before she gets here."

I pulled myself up on my elbows, still snarling.

"Before who gets here?" I asked.

Mom high stepped over a Lego representation of the physics behind centrifugal force, then stopped in the doorway. "Aunt Sarin."

If you look east in the spring and summer night sky, you will find the "celestial strongman," fifth-largest constellation, Hercules. Unlike Orion, Hercules wouldn't have been afraid of a puny bug, because he pretty much spanked anything that got in his way. Leo the lion, Hydra the nine-headed serpent, and even Cancer the crab. *Crack, crash, thud.* Even in his constellation form, Hercules is socking it to Draco, his left knee planted firmly on the dragon's star head.

But it's over in Hercules's right knee that you will find a white subgiant—the 198th brightest star in the sky, to be exact—called Sarin.

Being in a warrior's knee sort of fits my aunt Sarin. She is sturdy and tough, doesn't take a lot of guff from anyone, and supports the whole family. If anyone has something they need, they go to Sarin. And she always says yes, because she's reliable like that.

"I thought she was having a baby," I yelled, but my mom had already left the room. I'd overheard Mom talking on the phone to Aunt Sarin two nights before, and Mom had said something like, "*You're gonna have that sweet pea any minute now.*" I guess I'd thought she really meant any *minute* now and not any *day* now. Why people hardly ever said what they really meant was something I would never understand.

I got up and dressed, taking a quick peek outside to see if Mr. Death was maybe doing something normal like mowing the lawn or putting water in the scaly bird bath Widow Feldman had left in the backyard when she moved out, but no such luck. As usual, his yard was empty, his curtains shut tight, his house as buttoned up as Widow Feldman's housecoat.

I went downstairs and the first thing I noticed was the giant suitcase. And by "noticed," I mean stubbed my toe on, because it was literally sitting right at the bottom of the staircase, with two rogue pairs of shoes and a hairbrush resting on top. Tripp would have totally wiped out if he'd been there.

I stepped around the suitcase and went into the kitchen, where Mom was filling a plastic bag with snacks.

"Where are you going?" I asked. "Why is Aunt Sarin coming? Did she have her baby? I didn't know we had Fruit Roll-Ups, can I have one? What's the suitcase doing out? Where's Dad?"

Mom held out her hand, stop sign–style. "Whoa. Too many questions. Here." She threw a Fruit Roll-Up at me. Strawberry. My favorite. Tripp and I once brainstormed a whole list of fruit-roll flavors that would be even better—bacon, cheese dip, doughnut, buffalo wings. But eventually we decided that you couldn't call them fruit rolls unless there was some fruit in them somewhere, and who wants to eat a banana-bacon roll or a chewy sheet of pomegranate-flavored buffalo wings? We considered renaming them *Food Rolls*, but Priya said that sounded gross, and she started counting off about a billion reasons why Tripp and I could never be trusted with our great ideas, and by the time she was done, we had forgotten all about the business of rolling food into sheets. "No, Aunt Sarin didn't have her baby yet. She's coming to stay with you and your sisters for a couple days while Dad and I go house hunting in Las Vegas."

I grimaced, trying to swallow, but the food got stuck in my throat halfway down. They were house hunting. In Vegas. For some reason, this made our impending move all the more real. "Oh," I squeaked.

Mom shut the cabinet and zipped the bag closed, stuffing it into her purse on the counter and looking at her watch. "Now, you'll be fine while we're gone. Aunt Sarin will play games with you like she always does. This may be your last chance to spend some time alone with her before the baby comes."

Even better, Aunt Sarin would come up to CICM-HQ with me. She'd flash the lights toward Mars and look through Chase's Mickey Mouse binoculars and would swear she saw movement—a boat on a Martian ocean, maybe?—and wouldn't call me weird or make fun of me. She might even help me rename it so we could make shirts.

Finding Arty's Real Terrestrials. FART.

Ugh.

"But don't you think Dad should make sure he's tried all the other jobs here first? Maybe he missed one."

Mom sighed and leaned against the cabinet. "Arty, we've talked about this . . ."

But she couldn't finish her sentence, because just then the front door burst open, and a wailing rainbow rushed into the kitchen at us.

"Oh, Ayyymeee," the rainbow cried. "I can't gooo without saying good-byeee!" The rainbow engulfed Mom under seven thousand layers of fabric.

"Hey," I heard behind me, just before someone bumped my shoulder. Priya stood behind me, her bracelets clanking.

"Hey," I said. "I thought you were at engineering camp."

"I'm on my way there now," she said. "But my mom was convinced that when we came back in four days, you would already be gone forever. She's freaking out about you guys moving."

I am, too, I wanted to tell her, but I clenched my teeth so no words would slip out. I didn't want to look like . . . like Orion. Weak, sappy, afraid of a wimpy little move.

"Devani," my mom said, pulling herself out of the folds of Priya's mom's sari, which she wore over a pair of fancy-looking jeans and high-heeled sandals, just like always. "We're just house hunting. We'll still be here when you get back from Lawrence."

Priya's mom stepped back and wiped the corners of her eyes. "I just didn't want to take any chances. I can't believe my best friend in the world is moving . . . away." With the word "away," she burst into tears, and my mom was eaten by a rainbow again.

My mom and Priya's mom had been best friends since we were born. They washed their cars together and they took us to movies together and they sat in lawn chairs and watched us play together for our whole lives. It was going to be weird to look out the front window of our Vegas house and find someone else sitting in the front yard with Mom. Someone not wearing a brightly colored sari and high-heeled sandals.

"I wished dry rot on you," Mrs. Roy said, stepping back and wiping at her eyes again, this time with a paper towel Mom had given her.

"Devani!" Mom chastised.

Mrs. Roy's eyes got big. "I couldn't help it. I don't want you to go. I wished dry rot and roof leaks and crumbling foundations on you so you'll have to stay."

I was bummed that I'd never thought of that idea. Suddenly I was wishing those things on them, too. Whatever those things were.

"Looks like they're going to be at this a while," Priya said. "Want to go upstairs?"

"Definitely."

We went up to my bedroom. I flopped onto the floor and fiddled with a few Legos, while Priya walked over to the window, grabbing a space shuttle model along the way.

"Should we get Tripp?" I asked.

She shook her head. "I tried. He's not home."

"Again?"

"I know. I thought Chase started to say something about practice, but Heave threw a huge water balloon at him and I didn't stick around to get caught in the crossfire."

I pressed two Legos together. "Practice? What kind of practice would Tripp be in?"

"Got me. Whatever it is, he's not saying."

Briefly, I thought about the types of things Tripp could be practicing. Sports? No way. Tripp was more likely to be used as the ball than to successfully catch, hit, or run with one. Maybe he was playing an instrument. The flute, or something else lightweight that he couldn't hurt himself with. But why would he keep that a secret?

Then again, maybe Chase was crazy. Tripp wouldn't be keeping secrets from us.

Suddenly Priya leaned forward. "Arty! Look!" She pointed out the window.

I got up and joined her. Mr. Death was outside. Wearing his hoodie. Carrying his bag and box. Coming out of the woods. He rubbed his eyes impatiently as he walked.

"Holy cow! He was out all night," Priya said.

"Just like Tripp's theory," I added, and this time she had no argument.

We watched him cross the lawn, pressing our foreheads against the glass as he moved out of our line of vision. When he'd gone, we were silent, unless you counted the beat of my heart, which was practically thumping across the floor with adrenaline. No wonder I'd never seen him come out of the woods—I'd never been looking for him in the morning.

"That's so weird," Priya whispered. "What could he be doing out there?"

Oh, I don't know. Murder, mayhem, torture... "Probably . . . barbecuing." I'm not good with spontaneity.

"Barbecuing?" Priya looked skeptical. "I think Tripp is rubbing off on you."

"Well, barbecuing is better than . . ." *Murder, mayhem, torture...*

My watch beeped on the hour, and Priya and I both jumped. "We should probably go back downstairs," she said.

I nodded and followed, hoping my heart would hop back in my chest on the way down.

When we got downstairs, Mom was once again wrapped in Mrs. Roy's sari. Or maybe she'd never gotten out of it.

"We have to go," Mom said. "Corvus needs a job and there just aren't many opportunities out there. We have to take what we can get."

"But can't you get something closer?" Mrs. Roy whined. Her gaze landed in my direction. "Look at them," she said, gesturing toward Priya and me with her balled-up, snotty paper towel. "How will they ever get married if you're so far away?"

Priya and I groaned in unison. Our moms had been doing this since we were in preschool and I announced that Priya was "my wife." The moms had thought it was so cute, they made a pact to get us married for real someday. *"Aren't they adorable together?"* they would croon, watching us play tag or look through Priya's telescope or chase lightning bugs. *"Like a little husband and wife. Oh, and won't we mothers-in-law have such a good time together?"* they would say. *"Won't holidays be so much fun!"*

"We'll visit," Mom said. She squeezed Priya's mom's shoulder. "We will. And you can come see us. When we have a house. Won't that be fun, Arty? To see Priya in Vegas?"

"Oh! A Vegas wedding!" Mrs. Roy gushed.

"That would be wonderful, wouldn't it, Arty?" Mom asked.

I opened my mouth, feeling heat surge in my face so hard it might have killed me if we hadn't been interrupted by the squeak of our front door opening. I let out a sigh of relief. Saved by the door.

"Don't worry, the cavalry is here!" a voice cried from the entryway.

"Aunt Sarin!" I heard, followed by the sound of Cassi's footsteps running down the stairs.

Dad came into the kitchen and dropped a suitcase by my feet. "Our flight leaves in three hours," he said to Mom.

"We need to go," Mom said apologetically, and Mrs. Roy burst into fresh tears and threw her arms around Mom again. Mom waved her arms through the fabric, trying to find a way out. She looked like someone who was swimming and got a cramp.

"Oh, man," Priya whispered next to me. "This is going to be one long drive to camp."

Aunt Sarin, belly as big as Pluto, lumbered in, both hands pressing into her lower back.

"There's my little butt-picker," she said, and ruffled my hair as she walked by. I heard a snort of laughter come from Priya. I sort of hoped an asteroid would smash through the roof and kill me at that moment. "Go, Corvus. You don't want to be late. We'll be just fine here. Now, go, go, go."

Mom somehow freed herself from Mrs. Roy's grip and grabbed her purse. "We'll be back in a couple of days," she said, slinging her purse over her shoulder. "If you have any problems, feel free to go to the man next door. I talked to him briefly this morning and he's agreed to be a backup if needed. Not that it'll be needed, of course. Everything will be fine. We'll call when we get there. Cassi has cheerleading at six thirty, and Vega is not allowed to have her boyfriend in her room. Oh, and don't let Arty skip his baths." *C'mon, asteroid, where are you?*

"The flight, Amy," Dad reminded. He'd carried the suit-case to the front door and was waiting there. The two pairs of shoes and the hairbrush had been dumped onto the stairs, forgotten. "Sarin has it under control. She can bathe Arty just fine."

"That's right," Aunt Sarin said. "I've given Arty lots of baths in his lifetime. Right, butt-picker?"

"I can take my own baths," I said, then cleared my throat and said it again in a deeper, manlier voice. "I take my own baths. I mean showers. I take showers now."

What do I need to do, asteroid? Paint a target on my head?

"We should go, too," Priya's mom said in a watery voice. "Come on, Priya."

"Have fun at camp," I said.

Priya made a face. "Oh, boy, I get to build bridges out of dried spaghetti and sit next to Britt the Smelly."

"Maybe he's not smelly this summer."

"He's smelly every summer."

"And remember to tell Vega's boyfriend to leave by ten o'clock," Mom called. Dad was dragging her down the front walk, griping about parking being a long way from the terminal.

Mom broke free from Dad and rushed back up the sidewalk toward me. She kissed me loudly on the cheek and hugged me. "Oh, my baby boy," she said. "You be good for Aunt Sarin. I love you!"

"I love you, too, Mom," I mumbled.

Dad slammed the Saturn's trunk. "Late! Late!" and Mom threw herself into the passenger seat of the car. She rolled down the window and immediately began waving through it. "And don't let Cassi sass you!" she called. "Don't worry, Devani! We'll visit! We will!" she yelled. "Sarin, you call if you need anything!" she hollered.

And then, just as Dad pulled out of the driveway, she cupped her hands around her mouth and yelled, "And Arty, make sure you change your underwear every day!" And they were gone.

Priya burst out laughing.

Dear asteroid. Now. Now is the time to kill me.

8

THE AUNT KNEE CONSTELLATION

Two nights after Mom and Dad left, they called to say they'd found a "cute little crackerbox house" on Celeste Street that they thought was meant for our family.

"Celeste, like celestial. Get it? Can you think of a more perfectly named street for your father, Arty?" Mom gushed on the other end of the phone.

Yes. Traitor Street. Giving Up Avenue. Will Never See the Sky Again Through All Those Lights Boulevard? All of those would be more perfectly named for my father.

"No," I said. "It must be a sign."

"It has a big backyard," she said. "Lots of room to play in."

"Comet bombs make it hard to play in the backyard," I said. "And he pees on everything that doesn't move." Once, Tripp and I tried to play hide-and-seek in our backyard, but Tripp was so still behind the shed that Comet sauntered back there, sniffed him twice, and hiked his leg.

That was actually pretty funny.

Which only bummed me out even more.

I would never get to see Tripp get peed on again.

So Mom and Dad went on about staying in Vegas for a couple of days to get an inspector to look at the house and see if their offer went through and blah blah blah. I honestly stopped listening. I was too upset to care.

I gave the phone to Aunt Sarin and picked through my dinner, pushing most of the food around my plate aimlessly.

The sun went down, and Cassi took off for cheerleading. Vega and the Bacteria hunkered over a tub of ice cream with two spoons in front of the TV, which left just me and Aunt Sarin. I went up to CICM-HQ and got out the contraption, climbed onto the eaves outside my bedroom window, and started flashing lights.

"Knock-knock," I heard behind me. I turned to see Aunt Sarin standing in my doorway.

"Hey," I said.

"Can I come in?"

"Sure." I scooted over to make room on the eaves next to me, but Aunt Sarin pulled my desk chair over by the window and plunked down on it instead. "You'll have to forgive me, but I'm not in top roof-climbing shape these days," she said, and gestured to her stomach.

I shrugged. "That's okay." I put the contraption down and peered toward Mars through Mickey's ears.

"Having any luck?"

"Not really. Doesn't matter anyway," I said.

"Why not?"

"Because we're moving."

She shifted so her arms were folded over the windowsill and she was resting her chin on them. "Arty, it's the same sky over Las Vegas, you know."

"I know," I said. "I mean, there will be some changes in latitude and longitude, so it's not technically the exact same sky. . . ."

"Okay, okay, point taken, Astronarty," she said, using her old nickname for me, a much preferable one to butt-picker, I might add. "You'll still be able to see Mars."

"No, I won't," I said. "Did you know you can see Las Vegas from space?"

"You can see lots of things from space," she said. "Can I try?" She gestured toward the flashlight, and I handed it to her. She began flashing toward the mirrors, aiming the beam at the sky, her brow furrowed in concentration. "You can see the Great Lakes, the Great Barrier Reef, the Great Wall of China. . . ."

"That's false," I said. "You can't really see the Great Wall of China from space."

She lowered the flashlight. "Really?"

I nodded. "Well, I mean, with a satellite or something you probably could."

"Huh. Still, the point is, you can see stuff from space. So what?"

"Yeah, but do you know *why* you can see Vegas from space?

Because of the lights. And you know what you can't see when there's a ton of lights?"

She locked eyes with me. "Stars," she said. And she didn't try to tell me I was crazy or wrong, and that was what I loved most about Aunt Sarin. She could spot a bad deal when she saw one, and she didn't try to make it into something good. Mom would have told me we'd see plenty of sky and then asked me if I wanted some raisins.

"What are you going to name your baby?" I asked, too depressed to talk about space anymore.

"I don't know. I was sort of thinking about Castor."

Castor, as in Castor and Pollux, the two stars that make up the constellation Gemini. Although the Gemini stars are technically supposed to be twins, Castor must be the pushy twin because he's the first to appear over the horizon at night.

"Castor's good," I said. "I like it."

"I thought you might," she said. "Did you know that a *Castor canadensis* is actually a North American beaver? Isn't that funny? Name him after a star and he'll get a little bucktoothed rodent for a side name."

"Yeah, that's funny." (Translation: Not to a guy named after an armpit.)

"Speaking of names, what are you calling your Mars operation these days?"

I hesitated. "CICM-HQ," I said. "But I wish I had something that spelled an actual word so I could put it on a T-shirt."

Aunt Sarin thought for a few moments.

"How about COMET?" she said. "Calling Out Martian Extra Terrestrials?"

"Aren't Martian and extraterrestrials the same thing?" I asked.

"Not really," she said.

"And, besides, 'extraterrestrials' is one word."

"It is?"

"And, traditionally, comets were seen as bad omens. Like, if you were a Chinese emperor and you saw a comet, which they called 'broom stars' in case you were wondering . . ."

"I really wasn't."

"Well, seeing a broom star meant you were pretty much going to be out of a job soon."

"That's not good."

"Or possibly die."

"Oh."

"Plus, Comet is my dog. And he peed on my magnifying glass, so I kind of don't want to name anything after him right now."

"Okay, okay, understood," she said. "Not Comet. Tough crowd." She thought some more. "How about SPACE?"

"What does that stand for?"

She scrunched up her brow, stopped pressing the flashlight switch. "Sending . . . People . . . Around . . . Celestial . . . Enterprises?" She looked pleased with herself.

I gave her a look. "That makes no sense. I'm not sending people anywhere. If anyone is going to be sent, it will be me, and then it would be Sending Myself Around Celestial Enter-prises. Which spells SMACE."

She grunted. "Okay. MOON. Manned Observation OperatioN."

"You can't use the last letter of the last word to finish your acronym. That's cheating."

"Says who?" she asked.

"Says everybody in the history of naming stuff," I shot back. I put the binoculars back up to my eyes and squinted, hoping to find the red planet.

She was silent again for a moment, and then she sucked in a great gasping breath. "BABY!" she shouted.

I didn't even bother to put down the binoculars. "Oh, what's that supposed to stand for? Boy Alien Binocular Yielder? That's terrible. It makes me sound like I'm the alien. Besides, I don't want the word BABY written across my chest."

"No," Aunt Sarin said, her voice all breathless and ragged. I turned and peered at her. She was wide-eyed and pointing at her stomach. "Baby! Castor is coming!"

9

THE CASTOR-OID COLLISION

The next twenty minutes were pretty much a blur of chaos. Vega and the Bacteria heard Aunt Sarin's yelp and came running up the stairs, the Bacteria's ice cream spoon still hanging out of his mouth.

"What's wrong?" Vega said. "What did you do, Arty?"

I tumbled in through my window. My shoelace hung up on the corner of a shingle, which pulled my shoe right off. The shoe thumped down into the yard, where Comet immediately snatched it up and took off across the yard with it.

"No! Comet!" I yelled, scrambling to get up. "I didn't do anything," I said to Vega, then turned back to the window. "Comet! Do not eat my shoe!"

The Bacteria stood on his tiptoes to look out the window, then chuckled in slow, one-syllable laughs around the dangling spoon. "Heh. Heh. Heh."

"Get me a phone. Call Uncle Manny," Aunt Sarin commanded.

Vega aimed her steely eyes at me. "Don't act like you wouldn't do something, Armpit. You do stupid stuff all the time."

"Heh. Dog. Heh," the Bacteria continued.

"I haven't done anything stupid in a long time, Vega. Comet! Drop it!"

"Hello? A phone? You guys? Someone needs to call Uncle Manny." Aunt Sarin grabbed her stomach.

My sister planted her hands on her hips and cocked her head to one side. "Using my eyeliner to draw a pirate mustache and eye patch on the dog?"

"That was Tripp!" I yelled. "And it was a superhero mask. There was no mustache. I told you that a thousand times."

"There was so a mustache! I saw it myself!"

"Kids, I don't want to interrupt, but I'd really like to use the phone now," Aunt Sarin said.

"No," I countered, putting my hands on my hips to match hers. "That mustache is Comet's natural facial hair."

Vega made an I'm-not-stupid face. "Dogs don't have natural mustaches, genius."

"Heh," the Bacteria laughed. "Dog 'stache. Heh."

"It's not an actual mustache, it's just his fur!" I yelled back. "Look at him!"

Together, Vega, the Bacteria, and I all turned to the window and leaned forward, craning our necks.

Just in time to see Comet gobble my shoe. My whole shoe. Laces and all, in one swallow. Gulp. Like a cartoon dog. It was unnatural and unsettling. And my only pair of shoes!

"No! Comet! Aw, come on! Couldn't you have just peed on

it?" Then, as if in answer to my question, Comet got up, walked over to Cassi's swing, and lifted his leg. Well, at least I had that little consolation.

"Huh," Vega said. "What do you know? His fur does look like a mustache."

"Would somebody pick up the phone and call Uncle Manny, please? I'm having a baby over here!" Aunt Sarin screeched, and we all turned, sort of surprised to remember that she was still in the room with us.

Vega went into panicky overdrive. "You're having the baby? She's having the baby? Why didn't you tell me she was having the baby? Oh no, oh no, I don't know what to do. What do I do? Where's the phone? What's Uncle Manny's number? How far apart are the contractions? What happens if the baby is born here? How will we get to the hospital? Should Mitchell drive you to the hospital? Should I call an ambulance? Baby? A baby? Right now, a baby?"

The Bacteria's mouth dropped open, and the spoon plunked on my carpet. He ran out of the room, down the stairs, and straight out the front door, shutting it behind him with a house-rattling slam.

Vega and I looked at each other for a beat, and then we both raced to the phone in the hallway. She got there first, and Aunt Sarin recited Uncle Manny's phone number for her. Vega started yelling into the phone, something about babies and ambulances and some other stuff that made me feel like I was going to throw up. If Aunt Sarin started doing half the things my sister was talking about, I might have nightmares forever.

I paced in circles, one shoe on, one shoe off, trying to remember aloud the stars in order of brightness.

"Sirius, Canopus, Alpha Centauri, Arcturus, Vega, Rigel. Wait. No, Capella is brighter than Rigel. Or is it Procyon that's brighter than Capella? Or is it Riccola? Wait. What am I saying? Riccola is a cough drop. It's Sirius, Canopus, Alpha Centauri, Arcturus, Vega, Capella, Rigel, Procyon, uh . . . uh . . ."

"Armpit!"

I snapped my fingers, stuck my finger in the air. "Right! Betelgeuse! How could I forget that?"

"Armpit! Stop talking about stars for one second," Vega said. "Get your things together. Uncle Manny is on the way."

"Oh," Aunt Sarin moaned as Vega helped her out of the chair. "Oh, kids, I'm so sorry. You should call your mother. Tell her what's happening, see what she wants to do. Go to the guy next door. Your mom said he'd help in an emergency."

Vega helped Aunt Sarin downstairs, and in minutes Uncle Manny's car screeched into the driveway. He ran into the house and collected Aunt Sarin, his hands shaking as he grabbed her elbows.

"Easy, easy . . . ," he said. He helped Aunt Sarin into the car and then glanced back at Vega. "You guys okay?"

Vega nodded, and Aunt Sarin let out a howl from within the car. Uncle Manny looked panicked. "We'll be fine," Vega said. "We'll call Mom. Everything will be fine. Go!"

But it turned out Mom didn't think everything was fine at all. I could hear her screeching into the phone from all the way across the kitchen table. Vega held the phone away from her ear, *okay*ing and *uh-huh*ing and *yeah-I-get-it-Mom-sheesh*ing, and then she hung up and set the phone on the table and looked at me.

"So basically Mom wants us to leave."

"Leave? Where are we supposed to go? To Las Vegas?"

There was a knock, and the front door opened, the Bacteria stepping inside. "Aunt? Kid?" he grunted.

Vega shook her head. "No baby here. They went to the hospital." She looked back at me, but she was kind of talking to both of us. "Mom and Dad are coming home as soon as they can get here. But in the meantime, we're supposed to find someplace else to go. Mom said she'll call Brielle's mom and Cassi can just stay there for a couple of nights. I'll go to my friend Anastasia's house. And you'll have to go to Tripp's."

"Tripp isn't home."

Even Vega looked surprised. "What do you mean, Tripp isn't home?"

"I've been calling all day."

"Are you sure? Tripp's always home. If he's not here, where else could he be?"

I shrugged. "I don't know. It's a mystery. He's been missing a lot lately."

Vega pressed her lips together. "What about Priya? I know she's a girl, but she hangs out with you and Tripp all the time, so she's kind of a boy."

"Engineering camp. She won't be back until the day after tomorrow."

Vega stood up and huffed. "Well, do you have any other friends who are home?"

I hated that we all already knew the answer to that question. And that we also all knew that my standing around puffing my lips out, looking up, and tapping my chin thoughtfully, like I was going through my long list of social prospects, was a lie. But that was exactly what I did. "Nope," I finally said.

"You're kidding," Vega said, swooshing her hair over one shoulder dramatically and stomping out of the kitchen. "Seriously, you can't even have one friend, Armpit?"

I followed behind her. "I have two friends. They're gone. It's summer, Vega. People go places."

She went into her room and began cramming things into a backpack, leaving the Bacteria to shuffle over to the pantry and scrounge for something to snack on while he waited. I stood in her doorway.

"So, what am I supposed to do?" she asked. "I am not taking you to Anastasia's. There's a limit to what a sister should have to do, and hanging out with her armpit of a brother at her friend's house is definitely past that limit."

"I'll just stay home," I offered.

She slammed a dresser drawer and laughed. "Yeah, right. Mom would kill me if I left you here alone. You'd probably fall off the roof and get eaten by Comet."

Nah, I thought. *Comet would never eat me.*

Of course, I never thought he would have eaten my shoe, either.

She went into her bathroom, where I heard more drawers opening and closing. Soon she came out, zipping her bulging backpack as she walked past me and down the stairs.

"You're just going to have to go . . . somewhere," she said. "Come on, Mitchell."

"Where?" I asked, but she and the Bacteria had already plowed out of the house. For a few minutes I just stood at the bottom of the steps. I would just stay home. I could handle it.

Cassi was gone, so she'd never know. Vega had bolted, so she'd never know. I wouldn't answer the phone if Mom or Dad called. I'd have the whole house—and CICM-HQ—to myself.

I liked it. No. I *loved* it.

I walked over to the table and crinkled up the potato chip bag, tossed it in the trash, and closed the pantry door. See how responsible I was acting already? This would be no problem!

Just then the front door swished open and Vega stuck her head in. "Let's go, Arty! I don't have all day to wait around for you!"

Darn. She noticed.

"I don't have anywhere to go, remember?" I said.

"Yes, you do. You're going next door."

I slumped. "To the Moneckis? Mr. Monecki always makes me clean out his lawnmower." He also once had me sweep out his garage and is always saying, "*Here, son, you wanna make a nickel? I gotta job for youse.*" There were so many things wrong with that sentence I never knew where to begin and always ended up doing some huge chore for him.

This was going to be a horrible couple of days.

I trudged upstairs and got out my Studying Stars Makes Me Brighter overnight bag from space camp. (That acronym would be ssmmb, which doesn't spell anything, either, so apparently it's not easy, even for adults, to come up with stuff that looks good on shirts.)

"Nope," Vega said, following me. "The Moneckis aren't home. You're going to the other guy."

I froze in place. The other guy? She couldn't possibly mean . . .

"No way. I can't stay with that guy."

She turned her palms up, exasperated. "There's no choice! What am I supposed to do? Leave you here alone?"

"Yes."

"I can't do that. Mom would kill me."

"She might kill you if you just . . . abandon me with him." *Especially if he eats my face.*

"It's not my fault you don't have any friends," Vega said. "Mom told us we could go to him if we had an emergency. It'll be fine. Let's go."

I crept to my window and peered out.

There was Mr. Death, peering back at me through his window, the curtains parted just enough to show his two horrid, creepy eyes. We made contact, and the curtains snapped shut.

My heart beat wildly in my chest, and I swallowed a thousand times, trying to get my breath.

Check that. This wasn't going to be a horrible couple of days.

It was going to be my last couple of days.

10

A SITUATION OF INFINITE GRAVITY

When I was little, I used to think a black hole was a pothole in the sky, sort of like the potholes in the grocery store parking lot. Dark and deep, filled with oily water and floating leaves and Band-Aids.

But a black hole is really more like a force.

Technically, a black hole is gravity. But not just any gravity. Not the gravity you and I are used to, the kind that keeps your toothpaste on your toothbrush and keeps you from floating out of algebra class. It is more like gravity times eleventy gazillion. Gravity so extreme it overwhelms all other forces in the universe. Gravity that is impossible to escape. Even light can't escape the gravity of a black hole.

If you approached a black hole, first your body would be stretched pretty much to smithereens. But that wouldn't matter for long, because as soon as you were sucked inside, you'd be squished into a tiny speck by all that awesome gravity. *Splat.* Infinite density.

That was exactly how I felt when I pushed open Mr. Death's door.

"Hello?" Vega called, peering into the darkened house over my shoulder. There was no answer, just the faint odor of cigar smoke and the hum of the air conditioner. She and I looked at each other, and we shrugged. "Hello?" she called again. Still no answer. We craned our necks so we were both peeking in through the open door.

There was a cough from somewhere within the house. Deep, guttural, rattly. It made both of us jump and pull our heads back outside.

Vega straightened and pushed her backpack up higher on her shoulder. "Well, he's in there," she said. "At least we know that much. And he grunted what sounded like a yes when I asked if you could stay, so . . ." She paused, licked her lips, glanced nervously back into the black hole that was Mr. Death's living room. "You'll be fine, Arty." The Bacteria beeped his horn, and we both jumped again. Vega turned and gave him a hold-on signal. She turned back to me and bumped my back with her elbow. "So go ahead," she said, though even she didn't look too convinced.

I took a step back. "No way. It's dark in there."

She pushed me again. "You have to. I already locked the house. You have nowhere else to go. What, are you afraid of the dark now? I thought you got over that when you were three. Come on, I'm sure he's really nice. Mom wouldn't let you stay if he wasn't." She rolled her eyes. "It's one night, Arty. I'll come check on you if Mom doesn't get back tomorrow, okay?"

Again, a nasty cough echoed from inside the house. I took another step back. "He's a murderer. A serial killer with a cemetery in the woods behind our house," I blurted out. "I've seen it."

She cocked her head at me. "You can't be serious right now."

"Or possibly a face-eating zombie."

She made a snickering noise in the back of her throat. "Now you sound like Tripp. Zombies don't eat faces. They eat brains, in which case, you and Tripp are both safe. If our neighbor is into eating brains, he's going to starve to death with you in the house."

The Bacteria honked his horn again. We looked back. He was head-banging to metal music in his car and had hit his forehead on the horn. He waved at us sheepishly. Talk about starving for brains.

Vega shifted her weight impatiently. "Just go, Arty. Mom will call later."

She raced down the sidewalk and dove into the Bacteria's car and they squealed away. And when I looked back at the open front door, I could swear everything around it—the flowerpot, the shrubs, the statue of a little girl with a watering can—was bending and distorting, the way stars did around the edges of a black hole. And just like falling into a black hole, I stepped numbly through the open door and into the smoky gravitational pull of Mr. Death's living room. I could feel myself getting smaller and smaller. By the time Mom and Dad came home, all that would be left of me would be the chicken-pox scar under my chin.

"Shut the front door, the air conditioner's on," a voice commanded from beyond.

My hands shaking, I reached back and pushed the front door closed with a soft click.

And was enveloped in darkness.

11

TERROR: THE ALPHA STAR IN THE NEIGHBOR CONSTELLATION

I stood for a long time in Mr. Death's living room, afraid to move, afraid to run away, afraid to do anything. I listened for him, but mostly all I heard was that raspy coughing, which he did a lot. And also the sound of a lighter scratching to life, followed by the smell of cigar smoke, which wafted into the living room in plumes. My fingers sweated and ached from gripping the handle of my duffel so tightly.

I sorely wished I'd had the time to write a letter to Tripp—something cryptic about how if I went missing, to send the police into the woods behind Mr. Death's house with cadaver dogs, and instructions to avenge me in some really cool way. And then I got a little lost in a daydream about Tripp going all superhero and hanging Mr. Death upside down from his toenails from the top of Cassi's swing set.

Tell me where you've buried him or I will unleash my sidekick, SuperTripp would say, and Comet, wearing a superhero mask over his eyes, would lift his leg perilously close to Mr. Death's forehead.

I was so lost in my daydream I forgot where I was for a moment, until I heard movement creaking slowly down the hallway toward me, and the smell of cigar smoke got stronger.

My heartbeat *kathunk*ed in my chest, and I looked around the room frantically. I changed my mind. I didn't want to be avenged. Avenged people were pretty much always dead. I didn't know much about what it took to be the first astronaut to walk on Mars, but I was pretty sure "alive" was going to be a prerequisite.

Finally, as the footsteps got closer, I made out the shape of a table and scurried underneath it. A few seconds later, Mr. Death's shadow came into the room, the glowing orange end of his cigar burning in front of him. He coughed, long and loud, like Bigfoot hacking up a bear who was hacking up a Volkswagen. With a bad muffler.

"You in here?" he growled, sounding out of breath. I said nothing. He waited for a few seconds. "You hungry?" Nothing. He moved down another hall, slowly, slowly. "Kid?" he said, but I remained tight lipped. Just hunkered under the table, shivering and wishing I had stowed away in the Bacteria's trunk or hidden out at CICM-HQ. And especially wishing that Aunt Sarin's pushy baby, Castor, hadn't chosen today to be born.

Stupid Castor. If I died here, it would be all his fault. I should have put that in a letter to Tripp, too. *Blame Castor,* the note would say. *Let Comet eat one of his shoes.*

Which reminded me . . .

I glanced down at my one shoeless foot. In all the hustle and bustle of everything that had happened, I had forgotten all about Comet eating my shoe. I was hardly an athlete with two shoes on—how would I outrun a murderer half-shoed? I wouldn't be able to, and I would die wearing only one shoe, which seemed like a very undignified way to go.

The creaking returned. I gripped my bag handle tighter and swallowed, peeking around the corner.

"I know you're in here somewhere," he said. "Too shy to come out, are you? Well, I'll get you out eventually."

The blood in my veins turned into icicles. I could feel it jaggedly bumping and jumping around beneath my skin. He would get me out? How? What was that supposed to mean?

"You can have the bedroom on the right," he barked, and then disappeared from where he'd come.

I waited until he sounded far enough away, and then I crawled out on my hands and knees and, carefully, trying not to hit any squeaky floorboards, stood up.

I looked to the front door and back again. I could just slip out of here. Sneak out unnoticed and run away. Go sleep in Comet's doghouse for a couple of nights. Sleep in the rocket ship at the school or in Mr. Monecki's gazebo or under the cloaking branches of Priya's weeping willow tree, where we used to hide out when Priya had swiped her mom's candy bar stash. He'd never find me at any of those places. Plus, those hideouts all had the added bonus of me staying alive through the whole night. Or at least allowing me a few minutes to write my avenge note to Tripp. Because that note was really starting to take shape in my head, and it seemed such a shame not to get it on paper.

"I don't want to have to run after you," Mr. Death called from wherever he was. "But I will. So don't even think about it."

My eyes bulged. It was as if he'd read my mind. How did he know?

"You can put your bag in your room," he said a few moments later.

I took a few steps toward the hallway, still trying to avoid making any noise.

I felt my way down the hall until I came to a door on the right. If I remembered correctly, this was the room that looked straight into my bedroom at home, the one where I'd moved the TV for Widow Feldman. The door was shut, but if I squinted real hard at the crack beneath the door, I could make out a strange dim glow on my toes. I reached for the doorknob, and gripped it.

"That door is locked!" Mr. Death barked right in my ear. I jumped and whirled, dropping my overnight bag and pressing my back to the door, only to find myself eye-to-terrifying-zombie-yes-definitely-zombie-eye with Mr. Death. I was breathing raggedly, trying not to hack up my own lungs every time I sucked in a whiff of cigar smoke.

"I thought . . . I thought . . . I th-thought . . . ," I stammered.

"Your room is the next one down," he said. He eyeballed

me for a long time, the circles under his zombiefied eyes radiating against his white cheeks. He brought the cigar up to his mouth and took a long puff. Then, with his cigar hand he pointed to another doorway just a few feet away.

Trembling, I reached down and picked up my bag again, then zipped away from the locked door. I practically dove into the room and slammed the door shut. After a few moments of waiting for his superhuman undead strength to punch a hole straight through the door, I pushed a small table up against it. Then I sat back down on the bed, keeping vigilant, hoping Mom and Dad would come first thing in the morning to rescue me.

This was going to be a long night.

12

THE HIDDEN UNIVERSE OF LIGHTS AND PRISONERS

After a few hours, I grew bored and tired of being in the dark. I wondered what Cassi and Vega were doing right then. Probably eating snacks and watching movies and having a great time that in no way involved worrying that every moment might be their last.

I snapped open the curtains, the ones that looked out onto our backyards, and let in a familiar stream of moonlight that made the room seem bright.

I spent some time picking out the stars of the Big Dipper. Technically the Big Dipper isn't a constellation but an asterism, which means it's too small to be a constellation itself. It's actually part of the Ursa Major constellation, but most people just like to point out that it looks like a giant pan. It's the one thing besides the moon that Tripp can consistently pick out in the night sky, so I don't bother to argue with him about it.

Then I got bored with the Big Dipper, too, so I opened my

window and spent some time harassing Comet through the screen.

"Comet!" I called softly.

He stopped sniffing and perked up, one ear lifted higher than the other as he tried to figure out where the noise had come from.

"Hey! Comet!" A little louder.

He hopped in a circle, still trying to find me.

"Over here, boy!" Louder still, and I added some smoochy noises for good measure.

He gave a confused look to the eaves, where he was accustomed to seeing me, and then spun in a circle again.

"Keep spinning, you shoe-eating mutt," I mumbled, and that, of all things, was what finally made him find me. It was, apparently, the worst possible dog torture to be able to see your master but not get to him. Comet ran to the fence and leaped and leaped at it, bouncing off with his front paws and spinning in circle after circle, panting and whining. He was in a real state.

"Yeah, well, it's what you get, eating my shoe like that," I whispered out at him. "I hope all that spinning makes you queasy so I can have my shoe back."

As if he understood exactly what I was saying, he turned, bent his head, hunched his back, and barfed up what remained of my shoe. Then he looked at me and wagged his tail proudly. My shoe lay in the grass, all slimy and covered with sludgy brown dog food.

Gross.

"You can keep it," I said, and shut the window.

I was about to pull the curtains closed when I saw movement out of the corner of my eye. Of course! It was nighttime, the time Mr. Death usually headed out to his place of eternal unrest. I ducked below the windowsill and waited for him to pass by.

I counted to fifty and raised my head.

And there he was, his face right on the other side of the glass, staring in at me with his evil beady eyes.

"Yow!" I yelled, startled, and crab-walked backward until I ran into the bed. I scrambled under the bed and let the dust ruffle block my view of the window while I tried to get the panic to subside.

After a few seconds, I lifted the tiniest corner of the dust ruffle and peeped out. Mr. Death rubbed his jaw a few times and then turned and walked off, toward the trees, where he always disappeared. I scrambled back to the window, watching him as he plunged through the thicket, a box under one arm and a bag clutched in his other hand.

At first I just watched the tree line where he'd been, half expecting him to pop out at me again. But when he didn't, I used the opportunity to explore a little bit.

The house seemed extra creaky around me, and even though I couldn't see anything but shadows, I was too afraid to turn a light on. What if he came back? What if the darkness was cloaking something terrible, like an embalming table for a kitchen table or a coffin for a couch? What if I turned on the lights only to find something grisly?

I moved down the hallway and toward the kitchen on my tiptoes. As I got closer, I could hear the hum of the refrigerator. Which was good because I was starving.

The kitchen smelled like lemon cleaner, and the carpet gave way to slick linoleum. I tried to make out objects by their shapes—a toaster, a blender, a microwave.

I gripped the handle of the refrigerator.

What if I opened it up and there was nothing but faces lined up on the shelves in plastic containers? Did zombies save leftovers? It would seem reasonable that leftover faces would need to be refrigerated, so if Tripp was right about Mr. Death, I was about to be in for a face full of horror.

But I was so hungry.

And, besides, I was kind of curious what a face in a plastic container might look like. Would it look like when Tripp smushes his face against the car window?

I took a deep breath to steady myself, paused for a brief second, then yanked open the refrigerator door with a primal scream.

"Aiiiieeeee!"

I stopped short.

Oh.

No faces.

Plenty of plastic containers, yes. Some bottles of soda. A cardboard box like the kind you get when you order takeout

Chinese food. Ketchup, mustard, mayo. The usual. What kind of crummy zombie had such a boring refrigerator? There is nothing terrifying about pork fried rice.

On the middle shelf sat a plate with a sandwich on it, along with some raw carrots and grapes, a little bag of chips, and a note that read:

Just eat it, kid.

I reached for the plate greedily, but my hand stopped midway into the refrigerator. Maybe this was a trick. Maybe he wanted me to eat it because it was poisoned. Maybe I'd eat it and morph into a zombie like him. Wait. No, that's not how zombies are made, is it? Boy, I wish I'd watched more zombie movies with Tripp. I wish I knew where Tripp was. Of all the nights for Tripp to pull a disappearing act!

I leaned forward.

It was roast beef. The good kind that came freshly sliced from the deli. Thick, pink slices spilling over the sides of moist bread.

My mouth watered.

There are worse ways to go than poisoned roast beef, you know.

I sat at the table and devoured every last crumb of that sandwich. And the chips. The grapes. Even the carrots. I opened the refrigerator again and, even though there wasn't a note attached, grabbed a bottle of soda and washed it all down, then belched a belch so loud and long I wished Tripp had been there to witness it. I felt so much better.

I got up, put my empty plate in the sink, and threw away my trash, then wandered back through the house, wondering if Comet was still standing on our back porch, waiting for me to come back. Or if he'd eaten my shoe again. Comet did that pretty often, actually—ate things he'd already barfed up. And once, when Granny came to visit and brought her long-haired, smush-faced cat, Miss Penelope, he ate something she barfed up, too. The cat, not Granny. Though I wouldn't be surprised if Comet ate human barf. He ate a whole shoe, after all.

Now that I was full, I was kind of sleepy, so I headed back toward my room.

But I couldn't help stopping at the door next to mine. The one I'd stopped at before. It was still closed. I put my ear against the wood and cupped my hand over my free ear.

Nothing. Not even the scratching fingernails of hungry undead.

I got down on my hands and knees and peered under the door. I didn't see much, except, yes, there was definitely a strange glow in there.

I stood up again and wiped my sweaty palms down the legs of my jeans. Earlier, Mr. Death had sure seemed like he didn't want me to go into that room at all.

But there was a glowy light.

And possibly prisoners.

Come on, lights and prisoners! I had to go in. It was against human nature not to. If I was going to just keep walking and pretend I didn't know anything about lights and prisoners, I might as well join Comet in his doghouse tonight and fight over his bowl of breakfast kibble in the morning.

I had to.

Slowly I lifted my hand and reached for the doorknob.

But before I could even make contact, there was a noise. The front door opened, letting in a stream of moonlight. Smoke roiled around a shadowy figure, which lurched into the house.

"That door is locked!" Mr. Death's voice cut through the night.

I jerked my hand away from the door and dove into my bedroom. I pushed the table against the door again and sat on the edge of my bed.

Where did he appear from?

And, more importantly, what was in that room that he was so afraid for me to see?

13

THE INTERGALACTIC ASSOCIATION OF I HEART FACES

I awoke in the morning, slouched against the headboard of my bed, my cheek smushed on the wood, a string of drool snaking its way to the floor. The curtains were open, and in the morning sunlight, I could see the whole terrifying room much clearer.

The bed was covered with a faded flowered quilt, the dresser held a few knickknacks, and an adjoining bathroom had a shaggy blue rug tossed on the floor.

Which is to say, not at all terrifying.

At first I wasn't sure what to do with myself. I went to the bathroom, brushed my teeth, changed into clean underwear, and then just stood in the middle of my room listening to my stomach growl. I wanted breakfast. I wanted to know if Aunt Sarin had her baby yet. I wanted Mom and Dad to come home. I wanted to be out of this house. I wanted to go get Tripp and tell him everything, especially how he was right, so right, Righty McRighterton.

I sat glumly on the edge of the bed. What if I never got out of here? What if even Mom and Dad couldn't save me? Would I just waste away and die on a flowered quilt?

Somehow I'd always envisioned myself dying in a much grander fashion. Like an asteroid would fall on me while I was in the bathtub or I'd die of excitement over having discovered a new planet or I'd disintegrate while being the first human to cross the two and a half million light years between the Milky Way and our galactic neighbor, the Andromeda Galaxy. Those would be awesome ways to go.

Slowly turning into a skeleton on a flower quilt was not an awesome way to go at all.

I could just see my tombstone:

RIP

ARCTURUS BETELGEUSE CHAMBERS
He did not die in space
He had only one shoe
He was an armpit

Shameful.

I busied myself by trying to come up with some new names for CICM-HQ, just on the off chance I should live to see it again. I had:

ALIEN: Association for Looking Into Exceptional Nartians

Nartians? No. But I did like being an association. Associations sounded important.

CLOUD: Contacting Life Outside USA Dimensions

But I was afraid that would make the other countries mad.

SKY: Stars Kinda Yellow

What the heck did that even mean? Only one star really looked yellow to the naked eye, and that was the sun. Stars were mostly blue or red, sometimes orange, but to us they looked white.

This clearly wasn't working. I couldn't sit in one spot all day. I had to do something. I had to get out of here.

I moved the table away from the door and leaned the side of my head against it, listening for Mr. Death. I hadn't heard any coughing or smelled any cigar smoke yet this morning. Maybe he'd gone back out to the woods. Maybe he was a late sleeper.

Maybe he was waiting on the other side of the door with his teeth sharpened into razors, a knife in one hand and a fork in the other, wearing a bib that read I HEART FACES around his neck.

I tried not to think about it.

I turned the doorknob, feeling my heartbeat in my fingertips and behind my eyes, hearing it throb behind my eardrums. I opened the door a tiny crack.

No needle-sharp teeth.

No silverware.

No bib.

I opened the door a little farther. Stuck my head out into the hallway. Held my breath.

Nothing. Phew.

I went back into my room and picked up my bag, then went straight for the front door and my freedom.

That is, until I noticed something different about the room next to mine. You know, the one with the lights and the prisoners?

That door—the one that stays locked—was open. Just a crack, but open, definitely open.

I slowed to a stop, wavering in front of the doorway, unsure what to do. It wasn't open enough to see inside. I gripped my bag tighter. *I should leave,* I thought. *While I have the chance, forget about the room and get out.*

But there were lights and prisoners and I might be an association now. What association can resist lights and prisoners behind an open door, I ask you?

I reached out with my fingertips and felt the wood of the door lightly.

What was in there that was so important to hide? What could it possibly be?

No. I didn't need to know. I shouldered my bag and took a few determined steps toward the front door.

But then stopped and looked back over my shoulder.

What if he had a kid trapped in there or something? What if he was planning to eat that kid's face for breakfast? Wasn't I obligated to save that poor kid? If I didn't and I saw some poor, faceless kid wandering around the mall later, wouldn't I feel guilty?

I had to save that kid's face.

And, you know, there was the strange glow . . .

I went back to the door and gently, carefully pushed it.

It swung open with a faint groan.

Just like in a horror movie.

And when it did, I saw what was inside. I gasped so hard I almost fainted right there in the hallway.

14

THE GREATEST (OR AT LEAST PRETTY COOL) SPACE DISCOVERY OF ALL TIME

My legs didn't even feel like mine. They were numb and weak and struggled to keep me upright. I took two steps into the forbidden room and felt along the wall for a switch, not even thinking about the light possibly attracting Mr. Death.

I finally found the switch and flipped it, and then gasped again as the room was illuminated.

Space was everywhere.

Model rockets and satellites, moon rocks in glass cases illuminated by black lights, articles about manned space missions and Mars rovers and even the Iranian space monkey. There were glowing stars on the ceiling and giant blown-up photos of Mercury, Venus, and Saturn. There were photos of moons I'd only hoped to one day see through a telescope, and of stars and swirling nebulae and comets streaking across a crowded sky. Draped on the far wall was a huge poster of Earth as seen from space, and behind it, on a mannequin, an official NASA flight suit.

No, that should be in all capital letters.

AN OFFICIAL NASA FLIGHT SUIT!

My eyes got all swimmy and I realized I hadn't been breathing.

I rushed over to the flight suit and let out a gust of air. The sleeve ruffled in the breeze of my breath and I got all swimmy again.

MY BREATH TOUCHED AN OFFICIAL NASA FLIGHT SUIT!

I reached out and stroked the sleeve with my fingertips.

I STROKED THE SLEEVE OF AN OFFICIAL NASA FLIGHT SUIT!

I ran my fingers over the name Maddux, which was embroidered in silver on the flight suit's chest. I only hoped some space dust might have rubbed off on me at that very minute.

I was so enthralled with what I was seeing, I completely forgot where I was.

"What is going on in here?"

I jumped, my hand falling immediately to my side, and whipped around to see Mr. Death standing in the doorway. I was trapped.

I opened my mouth to explain myself, but my brain was still repeating, *Touch it, touch the shiny flight suit* and wasn't working yet. Besides, I had no real excuse other than lights and prisoners and associations, and I doubted he would accept those as viable excuses for invading his privacy. Not to mention mucking up his flight suit with my earthy fingertips.

He took a few steps into the room, waving his unlit cigar at me. "You just go into closed rooms in other people's houses?" he boomed.

I shook my head. "The d-door wasn't cl-closed," I stammered.

"So you just invited yourself in. What have you been doing in here? What have you been messing with?"

I backed up. "Nothing, s-sir. I've just . . . you have an official flight suit, and . . . moon rocks, and . . . I really . . . you . . . I wish I had my other shoe."

He took two more steps toward me. Soon he would be towering over me and I would be pressed up against the flight suit—my idea of a dream come true in any other situation—and I wouldn't be able to get away. Just when I'd finally found something to like about Mr. Death he'd go and ruin it by eating my face. Figures. My luck always went that way.

"Yes, I have an official flight suit. And it's mine. Mine, you hear? Not open for grimy kids to go drooling all over. That's why I keep it locked up. That's why I didn't want you in here." He was waving that cigar around so much it practically nicked my nose, and I was glad it wasn't lit. Who smoked stinky cigars first thing in the morning, anyway? "Didn't I make it clear that I didn't want you in here? Isn't it enough that I let you stay in my house? Don't your parents teach you to obey your elders?"

I was nodding and shaking my head so much I was beginning to get dizzy. *Yes, sir. No, sir. Yes, I mean, no, sir. I don't know, sir, I'm getting confused, sir.*

He walked in a circle in the center of the room, ignoring my answers anyway. "I moved into this house for some privacy. I moved here to be alone. Alone, you get it?" He pointed at me with his cigar and again I nodded. "I tell some mopey neighbor I'll be an emergency backup, yeah, sure, whatever, and next thing I know there's a girl begging at my doorstep, and now here you are. So I take you in and what do I get? I get a snoop, that's what I get! A snooping snoop! In here putting your filthy hands all over my things. Reading my articles. Looking at my photos. This is not a museum. These things are not here for you, do you understand?"

"I th-think so," I stammered. "I'll just . . . I think I hear my sister . . . someone needs to feed Comet. . . ."

I bent to pick up my duffel and realized a moment too late that I had scooted right up against the flight suit. As I bent, my backside plowed right into it. I watched in horror as the mannequin tipped and swiveled on its round base.

"Uh-oh," I said.

"Watch it," Mr. Death said, only everything suddenly went slow motion, and it sounded more like *"Waaatccchhh iiittt."*

I lunged forward to stop the swiveling, but my timing was off. My palm punched the flight suit chest, sending the mannequin careening off to one side, where it collided on its way down with a pedestal that held a particularly intricate-looking model rocket. The pedestal fell, sending the rocket flying across the room. It crashed into a map of the solar system, ripping a long hole in the paper, and then clattered onto a very important-looking metallic thing with Russian writing all over it. The rocket knocked the metallic thing onto the floor, and bounced to the side, sending a crack snaking down a glass case that housed a moon rock.

In the movies, whenever something terrifying is happening in slow motion, the kid always has time to spread out a field of banana peels and marbles, balance some half-full paint cans on the tops of the doors, and rig a pillow to explode, blinding the bad guy with feathers so the kid can make a getaway.

In real life, you just stand there and hope you don't poop your pants.

The swiveling, crashing, flying, and knocking down of things seemed to take forever to finish. And then when it did, there was a moment of silence, just the whir of a motorized spinning galaxy in the corner, and both Mr. Death and I looked helplessly at the mess I'd just made.

And then he exploded. That part was in real time.

"What the . . . ? How in the world . . . ?" He dropped his cigar in a nearby ashtray and stormed to the broken case. "Don't! Touch! Anything! Else!" he yelled.

I pulled my duffel tight against my chest. "I won't. I didn't. I mean, I did, but I didn't mean to. I was trying to . . . Now I lay me down to sleep . . ."

And then a miracle happened. There was a knock on the door, and then Mom's voice floated in from the living room. "Knock-knock," she called. "Hello? Arty?"

Mr. Death grunted and left the room. I followed, pushing past him and wrapping myself around her waist.

She patted the back of my head. "Oh, goodness," she said.

She held out her hand. "I'm Amy, Arty's mom. Thank you so much, Mr. . . . ?"

Death, I almost supplied, but thought better of it.

He grunted again, not answering her question, shook her hand, and then sat down in his recliner.

She cleared her throat uncomfortably. "Thank you for taking Arty in. We're so sorry to put you out. We stayed the whole night at the airport so we could get on the first flight out this morning. I hope he wasn't too much trouble."

"He's nosy," Mr. Death grumbled. "And clumsy."

"Oh." She glanced at me. "Well, I hope he used his manners," she said meekly.

"I'm not exactly high society," Mr. Death said. Mom looked even more flustered, her fingers fidgeting around her necklace.

"Come on, Arty," Mom said. "We should get you home."

"And I'm not a babysitter, either, so I hope this doesn't become a habit," Mr. Death said.

"Of course it won't," she said, frowning, and then turned to me. "Okay, let's go home, let Mr. . . . um . . . let him have some peace. Thank you again," she said over her shoulder as we headed to the bright patch that was the front door. "It was very kind of you to let Arty stay with you."

"I didn't have a choice," Mr. Death called out. Mom shut the door.

"Well," she said huffily as we walked across the yard. I was leading the way, just happy to be free, celebrating Comet-style.

"He certainly doesn't have many manners to speak of, does he?" I ran a circle around her. "He was actually quite rude." I dropped to the ground and rolled. "I hope he wasn't that mean to you the whole night, Arty." I hopped in place a few times. Mom stopped and waited for me to catch up. She held my face between her hands and looked into my eyes. "Arcturus, look at me. I feel so terrible about having to leave you there. I had no idea he was so grumpy. Are you okay? Do you forgive me?"

And looking at poor Mom like that, her eyes droopy and tired, I felt a little sorry for her. I was free now—did it really matter anymore how horrible my night with Mr. Death had been?

"It was okay, Mom." (Lie.) "It was actually kind of fun." (Super lie.) "He's got an official flight suit in there. It's the coolest thing I've ever seen in my whole life!" (Truth.)

Mom let out a sigh of relief, let go of my face, and kept walking. "Wow, a space suit? That must have been exciting. Maybe he'll let you see it again sometime."

"I hope so," I mumbled. As much as I hated to admit it, that was . . . a super truth.

15

TRIPP IN OPPOSITION

Mom felt so bad about abandoning me with Mr. Death, she was doing practically anything I wanted. Except canceling the move to Vegas. Believe me, I tried. So instead, the next night I asked Tripp over for a sleepover.

Mom doesn't let me have Tripp over for sleepovers very often, because this is how they usually go:

5:00 p.m.: Tripp arrives.

5:19 p.m.: Dad has to find his hammer to fix something Tripp broke.

6:00 p.m.: Dinnertime, during which Tripp devours everything in sight while simultaneously ruining everyone else's appetites by talking about something totally not dinner appropriate, like foot fungus or the longest snot he ever sneezed out or how good Heave is at turning his eyelids inside out.

6:30–9:00 p.m.: Dad. Hammer. Various places around the house.

9:00 p.m.–dawn: Mom repeatedly comes into my room to tell Tripp to stop talking/stop bouncing a ball against the wall/stop jumping on the bed/stop making that noise/stop . . . just stop.

So normally I don't even bother to ask, because I kind of feel sorry for my parents when Tripp is around. He seems to be an awful lot of work. But I was dying to tell him about my night in the Death Lair.

He surprised me in my bedroom, where I was getting a head start on an epic fort.

"Hey," he said, hanging his head upside down over the fort entrance.

"I didn't hear you fall," I said.

"I didn't."

"You didn't?"

He shook his head.

"You made it all the way up my stairs and into my room without falling?"

He nodded, grinning.

"Are you . . . okay?"

"I'm great!" he said. He tossed his sleeping bag onto my desk chair and crawled into the fort with me. "So what's the big story?"

"I had to spend the night with the zombie."

Tripp's mouth dropped open. "You mean . . . ?" He pointed over his shoulder toward Mr. Death's house. I nodded. "And . . . ?"

So I told him all about my night at Mr. Death's house, from Comet eating my shoe until Mom rescuing me. I told him about the space room and the way Mr. Death had flipped his lid when I'd messed it up. Tripp hung on to every word.

"You think he's gonna come after you? Like, for revenge? Turn you into one of them?" He cocked his head to one side and rolled his eyes upward, letting his tongue loll out while he groaned, zombielike.

"Of course not." Actually, I kind of did, just a little bit. In fact, it was pretty much all I'd thought about since it happened. "Do you?"

"Nah, zombies aren't revenge seekers. They just go after the smell of fresh face." He lapsed back into his zombie pose and groaned louder. "Faaace! Neeed faaace!"

I threw a pillow at him. "Cut it out, it's not funny!"

"Faaace!"

I bounced a stuffed bear off his forehead. "This is very serious, Tripp. He lives between us, you know. He's your next-door neighbor, too."

"Yeah, but nobody wants to come to our house. My mom calls us 'neighbor repellant.' Yummy faaace!"

He made a move to grab my shoulders, his teeth bared, and in jumping back I knocked down the blanket that had been my fort wall. "That's it!" I yelled, and launched at him.

We wrestled for a while, until Mom burst into my room, looking panicked, holding Dad's hammer. "What's broken?" she asked.

We sat up, our faces flushed and sweaty, and gazed around the room.

"Nothing," we both said in surprise.

After dinner, we waited for the sun to go down and then took CICM outside. Tripp ate a Popsicle while I flashed the lights toward Mars, the buzz of the cicadas in the trees rising and falling around us.

"So where were you last night?" I asked. "When I was at Mr. Death's house."

"Nowhere," Tripp said casually.

"You weren't home. Priya checked."

"Oh, that. I was out."

"Out where?"

"I forget."

"You forget where you were? How does someone just forget where they were one day ago?"

He took a big bite of Popsicle. "I don't know, I just forgot."

This made no sense. This was strange behavior, even for Tripp, who was strange enough to begin with. "What are you hiding?"

He slid the last of his Popsicle into his mouth and fumbled the stick off the eaves. Comet caught it in the air and ate it in two chomps. "Did you see that?" he asked. "That dog is awesome! You should put him in the circus!"

I narrowed my eyes at him. "And now you're evading."

"I'm not evading anything. I'm just enjoying my Popsicle

while taking in nature." He gestured toward the woods and then jumped. "Dude! Look!" He pointed to the woods again.

At first I didn't see it. "You're just trying to change the subject," I said, but no sooner had the words left my mouth than it all came into focus.

The woods were staring back at me. Slowly, with shaking hands, I turned my flashlight toward a line of bushes. Two eyes glinted back at me from within a black hoodie, perfectly still and surrounded by vegetation at the edge of the trees. Mr. Death's cheeks rose with a slow grin when I lit up his face. Quickly, I clicked the flashlight off, my heart pounding.

"Is that . . . ?" Tripp whispered.

I nodded. "I think so."

"He's watching us," Tripp whispered. "Why is he watching us?"

"He's not," I said. "He's just . . . setting traps. Rabbit traps."

Tripp turned to me. "That's the dumbest thing I've ever heard."

"I know," I said.

"He's planning his next meal is what he's doing. He's scoping out the best way to get up here and get us while we're sleeping. Does this window have a lock?"

Suddenly we both became very interested in window craftsmanship. We climbed inside and inspected the locks at the top of my window, making sure they were secure. When we finally decided they could probably mostly keep out a zombie, Tripp went over to lay out his sleeping bag.

I clicked the flashlight back on and, trembling, shone it back into the woods.

Mr. Death was gone.

So was any chance Tripp and I would sleep that night.

Where was Mom with her hammer when I needed her?

16

OFFICIAL MISSION: BREAD AND JAM

When it comes to politeness, moms can never be trusted. My mom, in particular, was the politeness queen. She believed in all kinds of torture, like sending thank-you notes and giving the neighbors plates of cookies that you totally could have eaten yourself and bringing gushy gifts to your teachers at the end of every school year.

So when she handed me a basket full of freshly baked bread and some jars of jam, I knew something polite was about to happen, and I was going to be the victim.

"You need to take this next door," she said matter-of-factly.

"To Mr. Monecki? Why?"

She brushed flour off her shirt. "No, the other guy. The one who took you in."

"I just spent the night there. It's not like I was an orphan or anything."

She gave me That Look. The one where she raises her

eyebrows and dips her chin and which would work really great on a cop show where she was a crooked cop who was about to punch you square in the middle of your forehead. "It's the polite thing to do, mister," she said.

I tried to hand the basket back to her. "But why don't you take it?"

"Because you're the one who stayed there, and it's good for you to learn to be polite, even when you don't want to be." She pushed the basket toward me.

"But he's mean. You said so yourself."

"He's not going to hurt you. And maybe if you're nice to him, he'll be nice back." She gave the basket another push and gave me another Don't-Test-the-Crooked-Fuzz look. "Honestly, Arty, it's some bread and jam. Just hand it to him, tell him thank you, and come back."

I tried on the pouty face that used to work when I was four. Like everything else that used to be adorable but gets a lot less cute when you're no longer four, it didn't work.

"If you don't come back in five minutes, I'll rescue you," she said. "I promise."

I sighed—*dramatically*—and headed to the house of doom next door, feeling like Little Red Riding Hood about to meet the wolf.

I knocked on Mr. Death's door and waited. And waited. And waited some more. But just when I thought I'd gotten really lucky and would get to just leave the basket on the porch, the door opened.

"What do you want?" Mr. Death said. "Come to destroy more of my stuff?"

At first I was frozen. For the life of me, I couldn't remember what I wanted. But then, thankfully, my body moved all on its own, moving the basket upward. Mr. Death and I both watched it, as if it were floating magically between us.

"What's this?" Mr. Death asked.

"Bread," I said. "Jam. Mom. Thank you." Not the most sense I've ever made—a little cave-mannish—but definitely better than I had been doing. Come to think of it, I sounded a lot like the Bacteria.

"I see," he said, and reached out a gnarled hand to take the basket from me. "Well, I hope she's not expecting anything back from me."

"No, sir," I said, and started off the porch.

I was halfway to the hedge that separated our yards when he called out. "Hey, kid!" I turned. "Perseids meteor shower peaks tonight. You should look northeast after midnight. And turn off that blasted flashlight. You'll see more."

A meteor shower. Otherwise known as one of my favorite things of all time. If you stretched out on your back under a meteor shower, every time you saw one, it felt like space was reaching out to you.

In my worry about moving and what Tripp was up to and trying to survive living next door to Mr. Death, I had completely forgotten about the Perseids shower. Mr. Death had saved me from missing it.

"Thanks," I said.

But he had already shut the door.

The basket was still on his porch, but the bread and jam were gone.

17

THE SURPRISIUS METEOR SHOWER

I watched the shower in my backyard, Comet lying next to me in the grass.

About an hour after I got out there, Mr. Death came outside in his black hoodie and eased down onto the grass in his backyard, too.

When Mom woke me up a few hours later and told me to go inside, Mr. Death was gone. But for a while we had been under the same sky, enjoying it exactly alike.

And I still had a face.

The next day I left a note on Mr. Death's porch:

> Two weeks. Neptune in opposition.
> Tiny blue dot, but best time to see it.

Mom had her way of saying thank you; I had mine.

18

ASTRO OR NAUT?

I was bored. Tripp was missing again, and Priya was doing something girly with some of her girlfriends. Mom and Dad were busy filling out house paperwork. I'd rather be bored than hang out with Vega or Cassi. And there was nothing on TV.

But I was curious. I couldn't help myself. Mr. Death hadn't killed me yet. He hadn't even maimed me. And he'd given me the tip about the Perseids shower. Clearly he liked space, and I wasn't sure if many zombies were astrology buffs.

I wondered if he'd gotten my note.

I knocked on his door, and this time he opened it right away, as if he'd been expecting me. You know, like the witch in "Hansel and Gretel." Not a good thing to think about when you're standing on Mr. Death's front porch, by the way.

"Yeah?"

"Um."

"Um?"

"Um." Just because I was curious didn't mean he didn't still scare the power of speech out of me. "Um, I was just wondering if you got my note," I said. "About Neptune."

"I thought the purpose of leaving a note was so you didn't have to actually have a conversation," he said.

"Right. Okay. I'll just be going, then." I started off the porch.

"You won't be able to see it through those piece-of-junk binoculars you've got, you know," he said.

"I know. I'll just . . ."

I had started to say, *I'll just ask my dad to take me to the observatory to see it through the big telescope,* but then I remembered that my dad didn't work there anymore.

"I have a good lens," Mr. Death said. "If you're gonna pester me about it."

"I wasn't pestering you," I argued.

He shook his head and waved me off as if he was disgusted with me, and then turned and went back into his house. I started to head home but realized he'd left his front door open.

I hesitated. Was this an invitation or was he just forgetful? Granny forgot to do things like close doors all the time. But Mr. Death wasn't quite as old as Granny. Or was he? It was kind of hard to judge the age of a zombie. But he seemed to really enjoy slamming his door on a regular basis, so I didn't think he'd simply forget an opportunity like that.

Besides, he said he had something that could see Neptune. I couldn't pass that up.

I raced into his house and shut the door, then wandered a

bit until I found him in the space room, messing with a camera with a giant telephoto lens.

"Trespassing now, are you?" he said without looking up to see me.

"You left the door open."

"Snoop."

I ignored him. "You took those photos?" I said, gesturing toward a framed picture of a particularly bright orange nebula, curling around itself like a sea creature.

"What of it?" he said. "It's none of your business."

"I think they're really cool," I said. "I like space."

"I know. I see you out there every night, sitting on your roof, watching me with your binoculars. Your parents ever tell you it's rude to spy on people?"

I frowned at him. "I'm not spying on you," I said. "I'm spying on space. Well, and sometimes I'm spying on you, too, but only since you moved in." I realized how dumb that sounded—like he was worried I was some secret agent who'd spent a whole lifetime following him around or something. "And only because you might eat my face."

He stopped fiddling with the camera and gazed at me curiously. "You don't make sense, kid," he said. "What's your name, anyway?"

"Ar—Arty," I said.

"Arty," he said with a sniff, overenunciating.

I stood up straighter and crossed my arms. "It's short for Arcturus. The alpha star in the—"

"Boötes constellation. I know where Arcturus is." He squinted his eyes at me and huffed a few slow breaths in and out, like he was sniffing me. Like Comet does right before he eats something.

"Are you a zombie?" I blurted out.

To my surprise, Mr. Death laughed. Threw his head back and howled. It was the strangest thing. I wasn't sure if I'd actually said something funny and I should join in the hilarity, or if it was one of those demonic laughs and I should make a run for it.

"A zombie? Where did you get an idea like that, kid?"

"A serial killer, then?" I asked.

He pulled himself up straight to match me. "No," he said. "I am not a serial killer."

We looked each other up and down. He may not be a zombie or a serial killer, but he was still scary. But he also had so much cool stuff in his space room, scary seemed like a reasonable trade-off at the moment. "Where did you get all this stuff?" I asked. "Did you really take those pictures?"

He stuck the end of the cigar into his mouth and chewed on it thoughtfully, then took it out. "Yes," he said.

"They're amazing," I said. "You can see Saturn's rings in that one. Did you know that Saturn is so light it could float on water?"

"Of course I knew that," he said.

I turned in a slow circle, studying everything. He'd taped the hole in the map and gotten a new glass box for the moon rock. His rocket model was still in pieces, though, a tube of model glue on the table next to it. I gestured to the flight suit. "Is that real?"

He nodded.

"Who is Maddux?" I asked.

He clenched his jaw, then tipped it in the direction of an article clipped from a newspaper so long ago the paper was yellow. The headline read, "Local Space Enthusiast Most Recent Graduate of NASA Astronaut Training Program," and below that, "Meet Cash Maddux, the Young Man Who Plans to Be the First to Walk on Mars!" Next to the text was a photo of a young man proudly holding up a certificate and beaming, squinting into the sun. He had a crew cut and squared shoulders, but his eyes were definitely familiar looking. I looked from the photo to Mr. Death and back again, my mouth making an O of surprise.

"You? You're Cash Maddux?"

He gave a slight nod, almost too tiny to see.

I gasped.

Mr. Death wasn't a zombie. He was Cash Maddux. The astronaut, Cash Maddux.

I had been living right next door to a real astronaut all this time.

Wait. That should go in all capital letters.

I HAD BEEN LIVING NEXT DOOR TO A REAL ASTRONAUT ALL THIS TIME!

19

TOTAL ECLIPSE OF THE MOM

By the time Mom figured out where I'd disappeared to, Cash and I were sitting at his kitchen table, eating egg-salad sandwiches and talking about exoplanets.

"So we really know for sure that there are planets orbiting other stars out there, like Earth does with the sun?" I asked, a dollop of mayonnaise and egg dropping down onto my chin.

"Tons of them. I've seen them myself," he said. "We're finding new stuff out there all the time."

"Like what?"

"They found an exoplanet thirteen times bigger than Jupiter. It's so big, they're not sure what it even is," he said.

"Could it have life on it?" I asked, suddenly too excited to eat egg salad. Who could eat egg salad when aliens were a possibility? Come to think of it . . . who could eat egg salad, period? It was gloppy and smelly and left a weird texture on the roof of your mouth. "Could *any* of these exoplanets have life on them?"

He leaned forward. "You ever hear of Gliese five eighty-one?" he asked. I shook my head. "It's a star. A few years ago they discovered a couple of exoplanets around it. And some scientists believe there is life there. One professor said he's one hundred percent certain."

I gasped, unable to swallow the bits of egg left in my mouth. "One hundred percent? Intelligent life?" This was huge. To me, this seemed like the hugest thing in the world, and I couldn't figure out why everybody on Earth wasn't talking about it.

He leaned even closer. "There has been a mysterious radio signal detected," he whispered in his gravelly voice. "The planet is in a sweet spot, not too far and not too close to its sun. There could be water, and anytime there's water . . ."

We nodded in unison, our faces just inches apart. ". . . There is potential for life," I finished for him.

"No," Cash said, his voice so low I had to lean in even farther to hear him. "Where there is water . . ." I leaned in even closer. ". . . There . . . are . . ." Closer still. "*Zombies!*" he yelled, and lunged toward me.

I'd like to say I giggled and played it cool. But I didn't. I screamed like a four-year-old girl and flung my hands in the air, my egg-salad sandwich flying out of my hand and thwacking against Cash's wallpaper, where it stuck.

He, on the other hand, laughed like crazy.

And that's when Mom did her knock-and-enter thing again. Only this time I didn't want her to save me.

"Hello? Mr. uh . . . it's Amy!" she called.

"In the kitchen," Cash called back.

She came into the kitchen, waving her hand in front of her face. "There you are. I've been looking all over for you. You're supposed to tell me where you are, Arty." She said it in that polite company voice, but I knew that was just for Cash's sake. When we got home she was going to rip into me for making her worry.

"Sorry, Mom, I forgot."

"Well, I hope he hasn't been bothering you," she said to Cash.

"No more than expected," Cash grumbled.

"Mom, Cash is an astronaut!" I said, hoping it would soften her some. "And there's an exoplanet out there, it's called— what's it called again, Cash?—and it probably has life on it! That's what some professor said, right, Cash?"

Cash shrugged and took another bite of his sandwich. "That is if you can believe professors."

But Mom wasn't even listening. She was doing that uh-huh thing moms do when they want you to think they're listening, but they're really thinking about something totally different from what you're talking about, like onions or how a ketchup stain got on the living room ceiling. "Uh-huh, I see, that's very interesting, now come on, Arty, it's time to go."

I stood and came around the table. "But I don't want to go home. You heard me, right? About the exoplanet? There was this radio transmission and they think there could be water and you know what Dad says about anytime there's water on a planet. Cash has a real-life astronaut suit back there. A whole secret room. Remember where Widow Feldman used to keep her ferns? He's got moon rocks back there, Mom!"

Mom put her hands on my shoulders to steady me, because apparently it's possible to be so excited about something that you can be jumping up and down without even knowing it. "Arcturus," she said sternly, "we need to go now."

Dejected, I gave in and followed Mom out.

"Thank you again, Mr., er, Cash, for having Arty over," Mom said as she led me away.

Cash grunted in reply. I turned and looked just in time to see my sandwich slide a couple of inches down the wall and fall onto the table. Cash reached over, picked it up, and took a bite.

It was weird how just days ago I was scared to death about having to go to Cash's house, and now . . . I didn't want to be anywhere else in the world.

"That man . . . ," Mom muttered as we walked across the lawn that separated our house from his. "He's such a rude old cuss, I honestly don't know why you would even want to go back there, Arcturus. And to leave me wondering where you were like that. I have a mind to—"

"Oh! I forgot something," I interrupted. "I'll be right back."

"Arty," she complained, but I had already sprinted back into Cash's house.

I raced into Cash's kitchen. "Can I come back tomorrow?" I asked, breathless.

Cash looked up from his (my) sandwich and chewed slowly. Finally, he swallowed, picked up his stubby cigar, took a puff, and nodded.

"Just don't bring any water in with you," he said. "Unless you have a death wish." Again, he threw his head back and laughed.

20

TRIPP'S ATMOSPHERE IS STARTING TO LOOK WEIGHTLESS

This time Priya got to the rocket ship first. She was sitting cross-legged on top of the tires, though, instead of crawling inside of them.

"You were just disintegrated upon reentry, astronaut," I said.

She made a face. "I can't stay long. My mom is making me go to some sleepover at my cousin's tonight. Where's Tripp?"

"He said he'd be here," I said.

Just then we saw something moving toward us in the distance. Priya shaded her eyes with her hand. "Is that . . . ?"

"Tripp? On a bike?" I finished.

Sure enough, the object got closer to us, wobbling and weaving but miraculously staying upright, Tripp balanced on the seat as if this was no big deal.

Priya jumped off the tires. "This is a big deal," she said.

Exactly. Tripp hadn't ridden a bike in years. His mom said the health insurance wouldn't cover him anymore if he went anywhere near a wheel again. Or a bonfire. Or most swimming pools and some sidewalks.

"Hey, guys!" Tripp called, waving grandly. The bike trembled from the motion. Priya made a small noise and clapped her palm over her eyes.

"I can't watch," she said. "Let me know when the funeral is."

But he stayed up, pedaled over to us, and eased to a stop.

"What's new?" he asked. He climbed off the bike and stood, his posture so upright he looked like someone had hung his shirt on a hook with him still in it.

"You're riding a bike, that's what's new," Priya said.

"This old thing?" Tripp said nonchalantly.

I gave his shoulder a poke. "Why are you standing like that?" I asked.

"Like what?"

"Like you're having your height measured." I poked again. He barely moved.

"I'm not standing any different than I normally stand. Sheesh." He climbed up on a tire and immediately slid off backward, landing in the pea gravel on the other side.

"Never mind," I said.

"So what's the scoop on the zombie next door?" Tripp asked, trying again to get on the tire.

"You're not going to believe this, but his name is Cash Maddux. *The* Cash Maddux."

They looked at me blankly.

"Cash Maddux, the astronaut."

"No way!" Tripp breathed. "A real space man? Like Luke Skywalker?"

"Well, I don't actually know if he's ever gone to space," I said. "The flight suit looks pretty clean."

Priya made a face. "So was he, like, mission control or something?"

"I don't know," I said, and it occurred to me right then that I really wanted to find out.

"Can I just point out," Priya said, sticking her finger up into the air, "that, one, he is not a zombie, and, two, I told you so."

"Just because he's an astronaut doesn't mean he's not also a zombie," Tripp responded, and, for once, he seemed to have a point because Priya didn't argue.

"So he's normal?" Tripp asked.

"I told you so," Priya said.

I thought about how hard Cash laughed when he scared the egg salad out of me . . . and then picked it up and ate it. "I don't know if I would say normal."

"I want to see it," Tripp said. "The space room, I mean."

"Yeah, me too," Priya said. "Ask him if we can come sometime, too."

I was torn. On one hand, Tripp and Priya were my best friends, and I wanted to share my amazing discovery with them. But on the other hand, I was afraid to tell Cash when his shoe was untied, much less ask him to let my friends in his house. Cash didn't strike me as someone who would love a seventh-grade dance party invading his space.

But I would be moving away soon, and I wanted to spend every moment I could with my friends.

"Okay, I'll ask him," I said. "Sometime soon."

Tripp and Priya cheered, and we all raced to the tornado slide where we had rock races until it was time for Priya to go home.

After she left, I got out my bike and Tripp and I rode around the neighborhood until it got too dark to see.

21

THE DEEP SPACE IMMERSION

The dwarf planet Ceres. Vesta, Iris, and Flora—bright asteroids. The spiral galaxy M81. The Mundrabilla meteorite. Laika, the 1957 Russian space dog.

These were just some of the things Cash and I talked about as I sat on the floor of his space room. He was bent into a folding chair next to me, guiding me through books and magazine articles, photos from his days at NASA.

He told me stories about astronauts he knew and the discoveries they made. He told me the jokes they told. He told me about the fights they had, the findings they disagreed on, the achievements they celebrated.

I could envision it all. It was like being inside one of my dreams, only it was Cash's real life. I could picture a young Cash strutting through endless rows of beeping NASA computers. I could imagine myself standing next to him at the eyepiece of a giant telescope, the kind that made Dad's telescope at the university look like Chase's Mickey Mouse binoculars. I could feel the excitement of getting ready to hop into a space shuttle and launch into the stars. It made me anxious to grow up so I could just get going already.

I was spending every day with Cash while Cassi cheered with the Brielle Brigade and Vega and the Bacteria spent every waking moment with their palms fused together and Dad painted and fixed things to get ready to sell our house.

Meanwhile, Mom worried about "cleaning out" and "getting rid of things."

Arty's version of "cleaning out" and "getting rid of things": Pick up the obvious stuff, like your wadded-up Easter Sunday suit from kindergarten and the bucket of broken things you and Tripp spent an entire summer collecting. Kick everything else under your bed. Put the Easter Sunday suit and bucket of broken things back where you found them. The end.

Mom's version of "cleaning out" and "getting rid of things": Actually cleaning out and getting rid of things, with the help of your son.

I didn't want to clean closets with Mom. I wanted to talk about space with Cash. At first Mom worried about me going to "that man's" house, but after I "helped her" with a couple of closets, she stopped minding so much and let me go.

My Five-Step Process to Getting Out of Cleaning Closets so You Can Hang Out with Your Astronaut Neighbor
By Arcturus Betelgeuse Chambers

Step One: Groan.

A lot. And not the usual groaning, but really loud, over-the-top groaning. I-Think-My-Appendix-Just-Ruptured-Into-My-Throat kind of groaning. I-Just-Stepped-Into-a-Pit-of-Lava-in-Flip-Flops kind of groaning. Vega-and-the-Bacteria-Are-Kissing-on-the-Couch-That-I'm-Currently-Sitting-On kind of groaning. And don't do it just once. Do it every few seconds for at least half an hour.

Step Two: Find Treasures.

And I don't mean real treasures like gold coins or jewels or Dad's lost golf shoes. Find "treasures" like a hair wad left over from when Cassi cleaned out her hairbrush or things kicked out of the old hamster cage or a muddy sock or a plate with a shriveled month-old hot dog stuck to it. Hug the treasure to your chest, make happy crying sounds, and tell your mom you'd rather die of an appendix rupturing into your throat while stepping into a lava pit in flip-flops than get rid of this long-lost gift.

Step Three: Guilt It Up.

When your mom balks about keeping your treasures, get sentimental about it. Tell her that she taught you to be sensitive and that you thought she, of anyone, would understand the significance of that particular receipt wrapped around that particular petrified hunk of chewed gum, because it was chewed "on that day," "when that thing happened," and when you both "laughed/cried/cheered/danced/giggled/ sniffled/sighed" over it. Together. Be vague. You don't want to accidentally end up in some big sentimental cry-fest with your mom about something terrible like when you were a baby and she used to give you baths and your cute little butt fit right into the palm of her hand. Embarrassville.

Step Four: Ask Tons of Questions.

Because once moms are in an I-Have-Only-One-Hour-to-Clean-Every-Closet-in-the-House sort of mood, they really love being sidetracked by questions like, "Hey, what's this?" and "Do you see that tiny speck right there? There. Right there. You can't see it? What is it? It smells bad. Can you smell it?" Or especially, "Is that mouse supposed to be in here?"

Step Five: Make the Pile Bigger.

And, finally, when you've worn her out with questions and crying and a fake spotted mouse, start putting more things into the closet when she's not looking. If she notices and yells at you, just let your lip quiver and tell her you were simply trying to help.

She'll feel sorry for you.

And next thing you know, you'll be sitting on the floor of the space room in "that man's house," eating a sausage log and flipping through a book about telescopes.

Works every time.

"Cash?" I asked one afternoon. I was wearing a space helmet and playing with a plastic solar system model.

"Huh?" he asked from his chair. He had a photo album spread across his lap and was turning the pages slowly.

"Cash?" I repeated.

"I said what."

"Did you ever go into space?" I'd already asked Cash this question roughly nine billion times, but he never answered me. He always changed the subject or completely ignored me, like I'd never asked anything at all.

Once again, he didn't answer, and all I could hear was the sound of pages flipping slowly, slowly. I decided to try again, because I really, really had to know.

"Cash?" I repeated.

"I heard you," he said. "And, no, I didn't."

I spun the earth on its axis. "Why not? Were you afraid?"

He grunted. "I'm not afraid of anything. Never have been."

I spun the earth faster. "Motion sickness?"

"Of course not."

I stopped the earth with my finger and laid back so I was looking right up his nose. Not a pretty sight, by the way. I wouldn't recommend it. "So why didn't you?"

He snapped the book closed and held it on his lap. "Because of Herbert Swanschbaum," he said.

"Isn't that an ice cream company?"

He shook his head. "Of course not. An ice cream company. I never understand a thing you say, kid."

He got up and put the photo album back on its shelf, then shuffled out the door. I didn't want to leave the space room, but I had a feeling Cash wasn't done talking about Herbert Swanschbaum, the non-ice-cream-company-guy, and I had an even bigger feeling that I was supposed to follow him so he could finish the story.

I found him in the living room, slouched into an old recliner. He had a newly lit cigar between two fingers. I hated those cigars, and I didn't understand why he smoked them if they made him cough so much. But I was afraid to say anything to him about it—you never knew if Cash would invite you to leave his house forever.

I sank to my knees on the floor a few feet away from him. I hadn't bothered to take the helmet off yet, and my voice sounded echoey. Which was cool. I wanted to make noises, talk, quote some *Star Wars* lines.

"Commander(er-er), tear this ship apart until you find those plans(ans-ans)! And bring me all passengers(ers-ers), I want them ALIVE(ive-ive)!"

"What?" Cash said.

I blinked. "What?"

"What did you just say?"

I felt my skin get hot under the helmet. "Oh. Sorry. I didn't realize I was saying it out loud. Just . . . some *Star Wars* . . . nevermind. Who is Herbert Slapschlinger?"

"Who?"

"Hubert Slapsnotter?"

Cash looked impatient. "Not Slapsnotter, Swanschbaumer. Herbert Swanschbaumer. And he was an astronaut. Went through training with me. We were friends."

"What happened to him?" I asked.

Cash puffed on his cigar. "Last I heard he's living in a retirement community outside of Port Canaveral with his wife, Rita."

"And?" I asked.

Cash let out a sigh. "Herb was better than me at everything. If I got a plaque, he got a medal. If a pilot requested me in the simulator, two pilots requested him. When his head was clear, I was panicking. When I was dizzy, he was steady as a rock. Heck, even when he was getting married, my girlfriend was breaking it off with me. Everything he had, I didn't. Everything I wanted, he had. I despised Herbert Swanschbaumer."

"I thought you just said you were friends."

"You gotta understand, kid. Sometimes there's a fine line between friendship and hate. Sometimes you can admire someone so much you start to think you're nothing because you're not like them."

Hating your friend? I thought about Tripp, whose finest moment involved shoving two green olives up his nose so far he had to go to the emergency room to have them pulled out. And then he brought them to school, put them on his burger . . . and ate them. It's hard to be jealous of that.

Cash continued. "Herbert and I weren't just friends, you see. We were both training to be mission specialists. The space program was big back then. You went into astronautics because you planned to go into space. We both wanted it. And long story short, Herb got it. He passed all his tests with flying colors, and I had high blood pressure. Game over for an astronaut. My name never got called. I stayed grounded from the day I signed on until the day I retired. The end."

"That's it?"

"That's it."

"So you never got to go?"

"And never will."

"Because of one test."

He nodded. "It's a cruel world, kid."

It seemed like a very cruel world to me. A world in which you can dedicate your whole life to the skies and never get to see them up close just because you failed one little test. What kind of things could keep me out of space? What things could keep me from actually meeting the Martians I would eventually make contact with in CICM-HQ? Who would steal my spot on the shuttles, who would steal my bunk in the space station? Who would be my Helmer Schwansmeller?

"That doesn't seem fair," I said.

Cash shrugged. "Life isn't fair. Doesn't matter now. I'm an old man."

"But what about your dreams?" I said, feeling fairly outraged now. I wanted to make him feel better with a perfect, echoey *Star Wars* quote, but all that came to mind was *"Into the garbage chute, fly boy!"* which didn't really seem all that appropriate for the situation.

At first he didn't answer. But then he shifted and leaned forward so his elbows were on his knees, his hands dangling between them, the cigar forgotten between his fingers. He looked me straight in the eyes.

"Can you keep a secret?" he asked.

I pulled off my space helmet so he could see me nodding.

"Okay," he said. "Come back here tonight."

"Why?"

He sat back again. "You ask too many questions, kid. Just come back tonight. You want to know where I go when you're up there on your roof, don't you?"

A chill ran down my spine. "Yes! Well, no. I'm not sure, actually. You're not hungry for a face or anything, are you?"

He stubbed out his cigar in an ashtray on the table next to his recliner, then stood up and headed back toward his bedroom. I heard the door close with a sharp click, and I understood this to mean that we were done talking about missions and dreams and goody-goody Herbie Snotbagger.

I took the helmet back to the space room and placed it back on the shelf where it belonged.

I patted the helmet. "You're all clear, kid, now let's blow this thing and go home(ome-ome)," I whispered. I went back to my house, nervous and excited for the sun to fall so I could come back and see Cash Maddux's secret in person.

22

BLASTOFF INTO NOTHINGNESS

"Hey, Arty, where you going?" my dad asked as I walked past him. He was perched on a stepladder, painting the last few inches of the ceiling over our front porch. He'd been out there since right after dinner, trying to finish it before the sun went down. *"So many things to fix on this old place before we move,"* he'd said, and I'd immediately lost my appetite. I hated thinking about the move.

"Over to Cash's house," I said. "We're going to . . ." I paused, unsure how to finish the sentence, because I really didn't know what we were going to do. I finally decided on ending it with, "You know. Space stuff."

The bald dome of my dad's head was covered with big baby blue paint droplets, making his head look like an Easter egg. He frowned at me. "Your mother says he's not a very nice guy."

Okay, maybe he wasn't the *nicest*. Nobody could argue

that. Cash was one angry astronaut. And most of the time I wasn't sure if he liked me or wished I would go away. But I didn't care. "He's okay," I said. As far as I was concerned, the "astronaut" part of "angry astronaut" canceled out the "angry" part. "He can be nice. Sometimes."

Dad's eyebrows raised. "That so?"

I nodded. "And we have a lot in common. He loves space like you and me, Dad."

"Huh," Dad said.

I watched him slide the last brush stroke of paint onto the ceiling. As if to celebrate being done, a fat paint blot fell and dripped down right between his eyebrows. "Dad?"

"Yeah, buddy?" he asked, distractedly scraping the brush against the edge of the paint can to squeeze off the leftovers.

"Is your observatory in Las Vegas going to be as good as the one here?"

He didn't answer right away. Instead, he came down the ladder and set the paint can on the top step, covered it with its metal lid, and rested the paintbrush across the top. When I started to think maybe he wouldn't answer my question at all, he sighed and leaned against the ladder. "I won't be working in an observatory, Arty," he said. "I'm working in an IT department. You know . . . computers," he said. He tried to make the last word sound exciting, like any old technology was just as good as space technology.

But it didn't work. My heart startled, limped, and fell into my stomach. "No observatory?" I croaked. "We're moving all the way to Las Vegas to work on computers? They have computers right here in Liberty!"

"But no jobs," he said. "Not for me, anyway. This job pays more, Arty. And we'll find an observatory in Vegas once we get settled in. We'll visit that one every now and then." He reached for me, but I ducked away from his hand.

"Find an observatory once we get settled in? Every now and then? But what about Mars?"

"Arty, you'll have plenty of chances to see Mars next year."

"But it's only in opposition one day!" This was true. Mars was visible in the night sky much of the year, if you had the right equipment to find it. But it would be most visible when it was in opposition, meaning Earth was between Mars and the sun, so the red planet was both the closest and also stayed in the sky the longest on that day. That day would be my best hope in communicating with the life there. No big deal. Only an entire three years of grueling work, gone. No problem.

"And we'll do our best to get to an observatory that day, Arty. You know, this isn't the end of the world."

But to me it seemed pretty close to the end of the world. The end of my world, anyway. The end of the world that I had spent my whole life dreaming about. How could Dad do this to me? He was the one who made me love space. How could he rip it away from me like this? Without even asking me! Without even caring!

"What happened to you?" I asked, my lower lip beginning to tremble, which was embarrassing because it meant I was about to cry. I glanced over my shoulder to make sure nobody I knew was around to witness me losing it. "You used to love space."

Dad sighed again and closed his eyes. "I do love space, Arcturus," he said. "But I love my family more. And this is what I have to do for my family." I thought maybe I saw his lower lip tremble a little, too, and I felt a little better about mine. If I was going to lose it and be a big bawling baby, at least I wasn't going to be alone about it.

Finally, Dad picked up the can by its metal handle. "Don't stay out too long," he said, all business again. "It'll be getting dark pretty soon."

I could barely make myself talk. "Actually, I was kind of wondering if I could stay out a while," I said. "I think we might look at some stars." At least I hoped that was what we were going to do.

Dad looked up and nodded. "It's a clear night for it," he said. "Okay. But you promise me you'll come home if you have any problems with him?"

"I promise," I said. "I'll be fine."

Dad nodded again. "Say hi to the Martians for me."

What would be the point of that? I thought.

Cash was sitting in his recliner again, just like he had been earlier in the day, only now he wore his standard nighttime uniform: black hoodie and jeans and a pair of boots. Next to his chair was a black plastic trash bag and a box. All of a sudden I was scared again. I knew that we were going out back tonight, and I still didn't know what to expect there. It was both terrifying and thrilling and, just in case, I tried to tell myself that a future lifetime zombie diet of faces could be quite tasty.

"About time," Cash growled. "I thought you weren't gonna show up."

"I had to get permission," I said, sinking into his couch.

"Something wrong?" he asked. He coughed, held up his cigar as if to smoke it, then changed his mind and stubbed it out angrily.

"Did you know we're moving?" I asked.

"I figured when your parents were house hunting in Vegas."

"Right. In Vegas. Away from my friends and from space."

"How do you get away from space? It's over your head all the time."

"But . . . the light pollution," I said meekly. "Never mind. I'm sure Mars will be in opposition lots of times in my life."

"Every couple of years," he agreed.

"Cash?"

Grunt.

"Can I ask you something?"

"Can I stop you?"

"How come you stay outside all night and don't come home until morning? I saw you once. So did Priya."

Cash ignored my question and swiped at the curtains to

peer outside. The sky was bathed in evening indigo. A lightning bug flashed. Night would be fast upon us. He pulled himself up out of his chair with a groan, then grabbed the bag and the box. "You ready?"

I jumped up, eager to go.

It didn't feel real, walking behind Cash through the dewy backyard. My teeth chattered nervously, and I glanced up at CICM-HQ to make sure I didn't see myself sitting up there, asleep, dreaming that I was walking with Cash through the backyards.

Of course, I wasn't there, but Comet was, and he followed us, jumping at the fence, his head popping up, tongue flapping, every few feet. When we'd passed the fence line, he danced around in the corner, barking and bellowing, as if to warn me that I was with a bad guy.

"I'll be back, Comet," I called, only half reassuring him and mostly reassuring myself, as the woods got nearer and my palms started to sweat. "Is there any poison ivy in there?" I asked, but Cash didn't answer. "Are there snakes?" Nothing. "Ticks?" Not a word. I gulped. "Open graves?"

Cash acted like he didn't hear what I was saying and plowed on into the trees, where a path led into the blanket of woods. I followed him, not sure if I was doing the smartest thing in the world, but I had gone too far to go back now. As the woods closed in around our path, I felt comforted having the moon as my companion on this walk. The moon and I had been buddies since pretty much the day I was born.

Even though it was a warm summer, the nightfall had turned everything cooler and the sweat on my skin picked up breezes that coaxed goose bumps onto my arms and legs. I listened for animals, but the only sounds I could hear were the echoes of Comet's barks in the distance.

I began to think that we might be walking forever. I started to feel far away from home. A nervous squickiness started to rise in my stomach.

"Hey," I asked. "How much farther?"

But just then I saw what looked like illumination between some of the branches up ahead. Not man-made illumination, but more like the blue light of a clear summer night sky.

"Is that where we're going? What's up ahead?"

"You ask a lot of questions, kid," Cash grumbled over his shoulder, but he tromped on.

Finally, he stopped, and I eased next to him. "Whoa," I breathed. "I didn't know this was back here."

23

THE TUNA SALAD CORPSE MOON

Before us was a huge clearing on a hill, which rose out of the ground, a rolling mighty mound of earth. From this perch you could see the farmland behind us, more hills, silhouettes of a few cows with their muzzles stretched to the ground, a sleepy farmhouse snuggled into a valley like a baby in a crib. Beyond the farmhouse, a pond, throwing the moonlight back up into the sky, looking like a slick of silver on the ground. I thought maybe I could even see the ball field way out in the distance.

Best of all was what was above us. With no streetlights or house lights or stop lights or stadium lights anywhere near us, the hill set the stage for the sky. The moon sat upon us, huge and marbled, and surrounding it were more stars than I'd ever seen before, twinkling and undulating, almost as if they were beckoning me. If ever I believed that something in the sky might be alive, this was the moment of proof. In that moment, I finally understood what Carl Sagan meant. I felt like starstuff.

I took a few steps and sat down, my neck craned. Suddenly I could feel gravity working, could feel myself being pinned to this earth by the motion of our spinning through the great galaxy.

Cash walked up next to me and stood with his hands on his hips. He, too, surveyed the sky.

I laid back, my hands behind my head, and watched the sky come alive, as if it were putting on a show just for me.

There she was, Ursa Major, the Great Bear, her back thigh the bowl of the Big Dipper and her tail the handle. I watched her lumber along, the stars her joints and rippling bear muscles. I remembered the old Native American tale about the three stars that form the Big Dipper's handle being three warriors who were chasing Ursa Major, her blood staining the autumn trees red. I'd known the story since I was a little kid, but I'd never actually seen it in motion before, not like this.

"I have a blanket," Cash said, and I jumped, having forgotten that he was here with me. He rummaged around in his trash bag and pulled out a ratty old quilt. He dropped the quilt on the ground next to me and then reached in again and pulled out some sandwiches and a couple of water bottles.

Aha! Tuna salad and a blanket! Not a dead body and instruments of torture at all! What was Tripp thinking? Wow, he'll feel really dumb when I tell him how wrong he was with the whole zombie thing.

Cash grabbed the box and pulled it open. I gasped again.

"Whoa! Are those Fujinon twelve-forty-D third generation with image stabilizer binoculars?"

He held them out toward me. "You want to look through them?"

My mouth hung open so long that my tongue turned to dust and I might have eaten a bug. I nodded. He pressed them into my hand. He might have just as well handed me a block of gold or a wriggling baby Saturnite or the keys to the International Space Station.

I took the binoculars and peered through them, training them on star after dazzling star. I pointed them at the moon, that great chunk of rock that hurtled around us, pulling at our tides, riling up our werewolves. I roved through the sky, looking for the red dot of Mars, hoping for the return blink of light I'd been waiting so long to see.

"Do you think it's possible to make contact with Mars from Liberty?" I asked.

Cash pulled his tuna sandwich out of its baggie and took a bite. "A good scientist thinks anything is possible," he said.

I lowered the binoculars and opened my sandwich. I took a bite. Much better than egg salad, and it had the added benefit of not smelling like the Porta-Pottys at the apple orchard, too. "I want to be the first person to discover life on Mars," I said. "I've pretty much devoted my whole life to it."

He met my eyes. "Me, too," he said. "But I suppose you've got a lot longer to prove it than I do."

We chewed, side by side, and he helped me find the teapot

shape of Sagittarius, pointing at the "steam" coming out of the spout—otherwise known as the center of the Milky Way galaxy.

"Cash?"

"Yeah?"

"Why are you doing this?"

"Doing what, kid?"

I shifted so I was facing him. "All of it. Why did you tell me about Hermie Schwanlaker and why did you let me in your space room and why did you take me out here?"

Cash glanced at me. "You ask too many questions, kid. Anyone ever tell you that?"

I nodded. Actually, yeah. A lot of people have told me that. "But why are you?"

He studied the sky for a bit more, and at first I thought he was going to ignore me again. "Earlier you asked me why I stay out here all night," he said. "And the answer is that I can't tear myself away. I know I should go home, get in a warm bed, sleep. But I can't make myself stop looking." He jabbed a finger upward. "Up there. Does that make sense to you?"

I tipped my head back and drank in the stars greedily. "Yes," I said. "Totally."

"That is why I'm doing this," he said. "Because it makes sense to you."

After we finished our sandwiches and our waters, Cash took the binoculars and placed them back in their box.

"I suppose I should get you back before your parents have my hide," he said.

Reluctantly, I stood and folded the blanket. I didn't want to go back. I wanted to stay out on the hill forever, looking through the binoculars and talking stars with a real-life astronaut.

But if I ever wanted to come back again, Cash was right, it wouldn't be a good idea to freak out Mom. She was pretty irrational about Cash. It was like she thought he was a serial murderer or something. (I know, I know. You don't need to remind me. But that was weeks ago. I was a kid. I could think crazy stuff.)

"Can I come back here with you again sometime?" I asked as we shoved the blanket back into the trash bag.

Cash produced a cigar out of his hoodie pocket and lit it up. He grunted and shrugged. By now I knew that was his way of saying yes.

24

MARTIANS, MORSE-SHUNS

The next time we went to the hill, I brought CICM with me.

We got settled, spread out our quilt, and unwrapped our sandwiches, which were corned beef. I brought a bag of potato chips to share.

"So I was thinking," I said, after we were done eating. I unzipped my backpack and pulled out CICM. "Maybe we could try to communicate with Mars together. We could be the first two people to discover life on another planet."

"Let me see that, kid."

Cash looked at my ragtag machine and suddenly I felt embarrassed by it, like I was carrying around something a kindergartner would make. He pulled and tweaked at some things here and there, moving the mirrors around, adjusting the magnifying glass. He pushed the power button on the flashlight and watched the beam sprout. Up on the hill I could see how there was no way the beam was reaching all the way into space. It was barely making it more than a few feet in the air. I felt silly for ever thinking it could make contact with a Martian.

"It's stupid," I mumbled, embarrassed, snatching it back from him. "Forget I brought it."

"No, no," he said, reaching for it again. "This is a good model."

"You had way better stuff at NASA," I said. I sounded pouty, but I couldn't help it.

"Yes, but that doesn't matter."

"Of course it matters. If NASA can't find life on Mars with all their equipment, how am I going to find it with a flashlight and a few mirrors?" I hated that this was the first time I'd ever realized it, that no way could I do what NASA hadn't yet done. What a dummy for thinking I could.

"You won't," Cash said. "But I like your idea."

My head snapped up. "You do?"

He nodded and fidgeted with the contraption for a few more minutes. "We've just got to make it bigger."

"We do?"

"I've got a spotlight in my basement. And I can get us some mirrors. Maybe even a magnifying lens. We can play around with it a little bit, see what happens."

"We can?"

He handed CICM back to me. "You ever heard of Morse code?"

I had. We'd talked about it very briefly in American

history class during our pony express unit. For a while Tripp and I tried tapping messages to each other during class with our pencils, but Tripp only ever answered with gibberish—ISBYKKQ—and when I asked him about it, he always said he got sidetracked thinking about playing the drums. And then Mrs. Hamill, our teacher, would get a funny upward crick in her neck and holler out, "Stop tapping your pencils on your desks!" and we'd have to stop.

"What if we tried to send messages via Morse code?" he asked. "That way, if we get an intelligent response, maybe it will be in the form of actual words."

"You think Martians know Morse code?" I asked.

"I told you, Arty, a good scientist thinks anything is possible until proven otherwise. Tell you what. Next time, you bring this little guy back here and I'll bring some other supplies, and we'll get started."

We talked a bit more about design, and I started to get really excited, like maybe this could really happen for me after all. Maybe, after all this time, my dream would turn into a reality. I, Arcturus Betelgeuse Chambers, Armpit of the Central One, would prove that there is other life out there.

25

THE HUEY DISCOVERY

A few days later, I awoke to the sound of Vega crying.

I followed the noise down the hall and into her room, squinting and scratching the morning away. "What's going on?" I asked.

She was hunched over in her bed, a dome of sadness, her face buried in her hands, a journal spread out on the bed in front of her. Across the pages of the journal, she had scrawled broken hearts with "Vega" in one side of the heart and "Mitchell" in the other. She'd also doodled "Mrs. Mitchell Bacturn" several times across the page.

"His last name is really Bacteria?" I asked, almost laughing.

"Bacturn, you idiot, get out," she said. "And stop reading my private thoughts."

Still. Close enough to be funny. Bacteria/Bacturn. Perfect.

"Sorry," I said, edging for the door. "I was just coming in

because you were crying and I wanted to see what was wrong."

Her face crumpled again. "Everything is wrong. Mom is packing today," she said.

I tipped my nose up. The smell of cardboard was in the air, and if I listened carefully I could hear the sound of packing paper being wadded and packing tape being stretched.

This was it.

They'd found their adorable Vegas house. Dad had fixed everything wrong with our crummy old house and painted up the ruddy parts of it. Mom had cleaned all the closets. It was only a matter of time now.

"How long until we leave?" I asked. I was really wondering, *How long do I have to contact Mars with Cash?*

"I didn't ask. A week or so probably. Which means my life is over." She leaned back into her mattress and started sobbing even more.

I walked to her and awkwardly put my hand on her back. I patted it a few times, feeling weird about comforting my sister in her pajamas. I did kind of feel sorry for her. The Bacteria was just a half a step up above amoeba on the intellectual scale, but he seemed like an okay guy sometimes. And she seemed to be really in love.

After a few minutes, I slunk back to my room and locked the door. Maybe if I just stayed locked in here, they could never pack it and we would never have to go anywhere. I could stage a sit-in!

But then who would build CICM on the hill with Cash? And who would flash Morse code at the Martian yeti? This seemed like no answer at all.

That night, Cash and I brought a whole wheelbarrow full of stuff to the hill. Cash had already toted up the giant floodlight and a huge battery that looked like it could power half of Liberty. He'd also brought some mirrors and a huge telescope almost as good as the one in Dad's observatory.

We hardly looked at the sky at all, we were so intent on building what I'd begun to think of as Giant CICM. Which, by the way, was only adding another consonant to the name, thus making it no better to have on a T-shirt than the original name.

"Hey, Cash," I said, wrapping duct tape around the corners of two mirrors. "Do you think my friends Priya and Tripp could come up here to see this some night?"

Cash grunted, which was usually his unhappy noise. But come to think of it, grunting was also his happy noise. And his thinking noise. And his hungry noise. "This isn't a playground," he said. "I'm not a nanny."

"I know, I know," I said. "And I'll explain to them that they can't come up here unless we're here and we've invited them. It's just . . . they've known about CICM since I started it with Cassi three years ago, and I think they'd really like it up here. They're my friends. I don't have a lot of time left with them."

It was the last part that seemed to get his attention.

I thought I saw his eyes soften at the words "don't have a lot of time left."

He went back to his positioning of the mirrors and grunted again.

"I suppose as long as they don't touch anything," he said.

I grinned. "Great! Thanks, Cash!"

We put the final touches on Giant-CICM and looked at each other, our hands on our hips.

"Well . . . ," Cash said, studying our work.

"We should try it out," I said, but neither of us made a move. I think we were both afraid that it wouldn't work and that all of our hard work would have been for nothing.

Finally, Cash leaned forward and flipped the switch. The light bloomed into life and caught the mirrors, which amplified it so far it turned into a pinpoint too small for either of us to see. Cash leaned over the telescope and trained the light at a particular spot.

"Got her," he said. "Got Mars."

We both crossed our arms over our chests proudly, the intensity and excitement over having achieved our goal too big for words. I felt excitement building up in my throat. I wanted to scream and holler, gallop in circles spanking myself, throw a hat in the air, flail on the ground and scoot myself in victorious circles. But that is the kind of celebrating you do only when you're alone in your bedroom. Otherwise people think you've been out in the sun too long and have gone all wonky on them.

Instead, I leaned toward the switch and started flipping. Four dots. One dot. Dot-dash-dot-dot, twice. Three dashes.

HELLO

Cash and I both stood, neither of us breathing, and then he bent toward the telescope at the same time I lifted the binoculars to my eyes.

Nothing.

I flipped the switch again. Four dots. One dot. Dot-dash-dot-dot, twice. Three dashes.

Again, nothing.

So I flashed the code again. And again. For an hour we stayed after it, and for an hour we got nothing back. Mars was a distant red glimmer and that was all.

"We should probably call it a night," Cash said, after a while. "Try again tomorrow."

I tried not to feel dejected, and even though I didn't want to give up—what if the moment we turned our backs, the aliens started flashing back their planet's history for us, in Morse code?—I knew he was right. We overturned a wooden box to cover the device and started packing our things away.

"It needs a name, don't you think?" Cash said as he gently placed the binoculars back into its box.

"I've been calling it CICM," I said. "For Clandestine Interplanetary Communication Module."

"That's a terrible name," Cash said. "You can't put that on a T-shirt."

We loaded the rest of our things into the wheelbarrow,

and I pushed it down the hill and toward the tree line again. "I can't think of anything better," I said.

We walked through the woods, the wheelbarrow getting heavier with every step.

And then, just as we stepped out of the woods into his backyard, Cash stopped and took the wheelbarrow from me. "Huey," he said.

"Huh?" Thinking he might have been going old-person bonkers like my grandpa Muliphein did when he suddenly thought you could take the Macy's escalator to a pizza place on the outer ring of Saturn, I pointed to my chest, Tarzan-style. "No, Arty," I said, enunciating slowly.

Cash rolled his eyes and cuffed the back of my head. "I know who you are, kid. I was talking about the doohickey on the hill. We should name him Huey."

I blinked. "Huey. What does that stand for?"

"Well, it doesn't have to stand for anything. It's just a name."

"And that name is Huey."

He shrugged. "Why not?"

Why not? I thought interplanetary devices were supposed to be named something inspirational, something exciting, something important. Like Odyssey, Discovery, Spirit, Curiosity. Not *Huey.*

But I kind of liked it.

"Sure, why not?" I said. "Huey, it is."

THE SILENT BUT DEADLY NEBULA

"Okay, before we go in, there are a few rules you have to follow." I stood at the edge of the woods facing Tripp and Priya.
"No running or jumping or wrestling or throwing your shoes
or dive-bombing or sword fighting with sticks or anything
else that might involve throwing things into the air. No loud
talking. No singing songs about burps. Or singing songs in
burp language. You have to act normal around Huey. Cash
won't put up with any . . ." I reached for the right words, but
realized the best word was, "anything. Cash won't put up with
anything. Got it?"

Priya nodded and Tripp saluted me.

"You sure this is safe?" Priya asked, her hands buried in
the sleeping bag she'd brought along. She eyeballed the darkness surrounding us.

"Aha!" Tripp yelled pointing in her face. "Who's not so
sure about the zombie thing now, huh?"

Priya swiped at his finger and he whipped it away and right into a tree trunk. He sucked on it. "I am totally sure we are not going to be attacked by zombies, Tripp. I'm more worried that you're going to tear down the whole forest on top of us. Watch where you're—"

But it was too late. Tripp, walking backward and nursing his finger, tripped over a tree root. But to our surprise, he didn't fall. Instead, he pivoted on one toe, stretched his arms to the side, did a graceful leap, and landed, his heels together, his hands clasped at his left hip.

"Did that really just happen?" I asked.

"What was that?" Priya asked at exactly the same time.

Tripp looked sheepish. "What?"

"You didn't fall," Priya said. "Something is up. First you're riding a bike, and now you're leaping over tree stumps and not falling?"

"And standing funny," I added.

"Nothing is up. I just got lucky," Tripp said, and almost to prove his point, he turned and walked face-first into a poison ivy plant that was growing up the side of the tree.

"No problem, guys," he said brightly. "I've fallen into poison ivy so many times, the doctor says I'm immune to it now."

Priya and I exchanged skeptical glances. "Come on," I said, "we're almost there."

Cash was already there waiting for us. I could see the flashing spotlight before we were even all the way out of the woods.

"Don't touch anything," I reminded Tripp as we hiked to the top of the hill. But Tripp was busy saying, "Whoooa," the same way I had said it when I first came to the hill. Even Priya seemed to be mesmerized. She clutched her sleeping bag under one arm and trotted to the top of the hill, gazing skyward.

"It's so beautiful up here, Arty," she said.

"Thanks," I said proudly, as if I (1) had made space beautiful myself, and (2) had discovered the hill, neither of which I'd actually done.

We spread out Priya's sleeping bag, and Cash enthralled them both by letting them peer through the telescope at the various constellations and nebulae he pointed out. We sat on our blankets and talked about Huey, about his purpose and our plans to be the first astronauts (yes, I knew I was lumping myself in with an actual astronaut, but I was sort of in the moment) to discover life on Mars.

After a while, we turned off Huey to lie on our backs across the blankets. Just looking, just talking, just telling star stories and pointing to things nobody else could follow.

"The moon is so huge from up here," Priya said. "It almost feels like you can reach up and touch it." She held her hands straight up into the sky, her bracelets clanking to her elbow. "Our science teacher told us that the moon was once part of Earth. She said it was knocked off in a crash. Weird to think we're looking at more Earth up there."

"I've heard that," I said, pulling myself up on an elbow so I was facing her. "Some scientists think another planet smacked into us and fused together with us, and the stuff that was knocked off in the impact gathered together to become the moon. They say the rocks on the moon have identical oxygen levels as we do here. They called it the um . . . the um . . ."

"The giant impact theory," Cash intoned.

"The giant impact theory," we all repeated at the same time.

"What I think is cool is the way the pieces that were knocked off found each other and came back together to form the moon," I said.

Priya raised her eyes to meet mine. "It's, like, even being scattered about couldn't make it forget who it really was. Maybe someday it will find its way back to Earth and become whole again."

Nah, it's actually moving away from Earth, I wanted to tell her, but something tickling the backs of my ears made me think she wasn't really talking about the moon anymore, so I didn't say it, even though I wasn't entirely sure I knew exactly what she was talking about.

"So what happened to the people who were on the parts that got knocked off?" Tripp asked.

"It was billions of years ago," Cash said. "No people."

"How do we know?" Tripp asked. "Could have been billion-year-old people on that thing, minding their own business, sitting around in their tightie whities, playing their Xboxes, drinking a soda, whatever, and then all of a sudden, *bang!* They're floating out in space. Ahhh!" He waved his arms and legs like someone flying through gravity-less space.

"There are so many things wrong with that scenario, I don't even know where to begin," Priya said. She raised a finger. "One, this was back when the earth was brand-new. There weren't any people. Two, Xbox, really? Even you should be able to remember a time before Xbox. Three . . ." She trailed off, her nose wrinkling. "What is that . . ."

Just as she said it, I smelled it. One of Tripp's silent but deadly after-dinner bombs. "Tripp!" we yelled in unison, both of us sitting up. Even Cash pulled himself up, groaning.

Tripp grinned. "Sorry, couldn't help it. Thinking about people being blown off the earth into space gets me gassy."

Priya jumped to her feet and began tugging at the sleeping bag. "Ew, and you did it on my bag. Get off! Get off!"

Tripp laughed, and I had to press my lips together to keep from laughing along with him. Something told me Priya would not find the humor in it, which was something weird that happened to her when she stopped being Priya and started being a girl—she stopped seeing the inherently funny aspect of bodily functions. "It was a re-creation of the giant impact theory," Tripp said, rolling over into the grass. He lifted his leg. "Kapow! Moon dust!"

"You shouldn't do those kinds of things in front of a lady," Cash said, though he looked a little like he was trying not to laugh as well.

"She's not a lady. She's Priya," Tripp said.

"No, she is a lady, Tripp," I said, and I wanted to suck the words right back into my mouth as soon as they came out, because I was pretty sure they sounded like *mushy gushy mush mush.*

They must not have, though, because Tripp simply tipped the empty thermos over his tongue to catch the very last drop of hot cocoa and said, "Pfft. Lady. Whatever."

But when I rolled Priya's bag into a tight tube and handed it to her, she smiled at me.

Kapow. Moon dust.

27

THE GROUCHYTUSH HYPOTHESIS

My house was becoming a maze of boxes. Mom kept out only the essentials: five plates, cups, and sets of silverware; necessary clothing; and, of course, the raisins. Every minute that she wasn't busy rolling our breakables in paper, she was stress baking. One night she even put raisins in the meatloaf. Which, by the way, proved incorrect my long-held hypothesis that meatloaf couldn't be made any grosser.

"When are we moving?" I asked one evening, pushing a plate of peanut butter raisin toffee bars away. The Bacteria leaned forward and grabbed one with his non-Vega-hand-holding hand. It was like the kid couldn't get tired of raisins.

"As soon as we're all packed," she said. "Dad's new job starts in a few weeks, and we'd like to have some time to settle in before he goes to work."

Vega and Cassi took one look at each other and started

bawling, the two of them rushing up to their bedrooms again, leaving the Bacteria free to fill a second hand with a cookie.

"I'll miss you, li'l dude," he said, which kind of made me feel a little bit bad about how much I wouldn't miss him at all.

So with the deadline being "as soon as we're all packed," it seemed like the best possible way to put off moving would be to never get fully packed. So I began sneaking around at night unpacking things. Just a few things here and there—a snow globe in the dining room, a stack of T-shirts in my bedroom, the toilet brush, the toaster oven. So far Mom hadn't figured out that she'd been repacking the same things over and over again, though she kept mumbling that she didn't understand why this was taking so long.

Now, before you go feeling bad for my mom, just remember that parents trick kids all the time. How many times have you heard, "This shot is only going to feel like a little pinch?" And how many times has it in fact felt like someone had ripped your arm off and shoved it down a garbage disposal and then run over it with a train? That's what I thought. Moving on.

During the day, Tripp and Priya and I would scrounge for something to play with, something that hadn't been packed (my house), or wasn't girly (Priya's house), or wasn't broken or stolen or being hidden down the front of someone's pants (Tripp's house). And then at night I would meet Cash up on the hill and we would fire up Huey, tapping out new messages. We tried the obvious:

.-- . / -.-. --- -- . / .. -. / .--. . .- -.-. .

WE COME IN PEACE

And the less obvious:

-.. --- / -.-- --- ..- / .-.. .. -.- . / .- -. -.-. .... --- ...- .. . ... /
--- -. / -.-- --- ..- .-. / .--. .. --.. --.. .- / ..--..

DO YOU LIKE ANCHOVIES ON YOUR PIZZA?

And even the downright dumb:

-.- -. --- -.-. -.- / -.- -. --- -.-. -.- / .-- .... --- .----. ... /
- .... . .-. . / - .... .-. - .----. ... / .-- .... .-. - / .-- . .----. .-. . /
- .-. -.-- .. -. --. / - --- / ..-. .. -. -.. / --- ..- -

KNOCK KNOCK
WHO'S THERE
THAT'S WHAT WE'RE TRYING TO FIND OUT!

"I don't know if we're ever going to find anyone," I said one night as we traipsed back through the woods. Our traipsing had gotten much slower these days, and Cash usually had to stop a couple of times and bend over with his hands on his knees to catch his breath along the path.

"You shouldn't give up on something you believe in, kid," he said between coughs, his cigar burning between his fingers. I had noticed that Cash had begun looking a little gray, and his skin had started to hang looser than usual, the whites of his eyes dull like eggs fried in bacon grease.

"Maybe you should give up smoking those things," I said, finally working up the courage to say what I'd been thinking since we met. "It's not good for you. They make you cough a lot."

He spat in the weeds at the side of the trail and glanced at me. "Come on, let's go." And we took off again, him leading the way like he was trying to prove to me that he could.

I got home that night and unpacked more things than usual, starting with a whole shelf full of bed sheets and ending with the TV trays that Mom had spent an hour wrestling just right into a box that afternoon.

She came down the stairs just as I pulled the last tray out of the box.

"Arty, what are you doing?" she said, and I whipped around like I'd just been caught stealing something. Which I kind of was. Stealing all her hard work.

I lowered the tray to the ground.

"Nothing."

"Yes, you are. You're unpacking those trays. Why?" She came into the room, gathering her pink fluffy bathrobe around her. She stopped and her eyes grew big, like something had just dawned on her. "You've been unpacking things. I haven't been going crazy after all. It's you."

"I don't know what you're talking about," I said, but I knew there was no way I was going to convince her when I'd been caught tray-handed. I sat on the hearth. "I'm sorry, Mom. I didn't mean to make you think you were going crazy. I just wanted it to take longer."

"The packing? But why? You like to see me work?"

I shook my head miserably. "I don't want to move."

"Oh, honey." Mom moved through the box maze and sat on the fireplace next to me. She wrapped her arm around my shoulders, and I couldn't help it. I nestled my head against her and closed my eyes like a little kid. "None of us wants to move," she said.

"Then why are we?"

She took a deep breath. "Because we have to. This is important for your dad, and a family supports one another through important decisions."

"But I'm losing everything important to me," I said. "Priya, Tripp, the observatory, CICM, Cash, everything."

She leaned away so she could look into my face, which I ducked, trying to hide from her. It was much easier to whine when nobody was looking at you. "You really like that mean old coot, don't you?" she said, and her voice was filled with wonder, rather than the irritation it'd been filled with all the other times she'd talked about him.

"He's an astronaut."

"He's a Grouchytush," she said, and I smiled, even though smiling tended to mess up whining efforts.

"Mom. He's an *astronaut*." I said it more slowly this time, eyeing her importantly. "And he's not mean. Well, not *that* mean."

She tucked her lips in on themselves and nodded. "I should have seen that earlier. He's an astronaut. Of course you'd love him."

I blushed. "I don't love him. Gross." But I supposed in a

weird way I kind of did. Not like in a gushing, slobbery way like Vega and the Bacteria, and not in the totally obsessed way of Cassi and the Brielle Brigade, and definitely not quite in the same way Comet loved Cassi's swing. But in my own way, yeah, I guess I did.

"Well," Mom said, patting my knee and standing up, smoothing her robe over her knees, "you have a couple of weeks left with all of them. Make the most of your time. Don't sit around moping before you're even gone. Besides, it's not like when you move away, it'll be the last time you'll ever see them again."

"Thanks, Mom," I said.

I guess she was right. There was still plenty of time.

28

TWO MOONS NAMED FEAR AND PANIC

There was a strange white car with Kansas license plates in Cash's driveway the next day.

I sat on the porch steps and stared at it, willing it to go away.

"Looks like your pal has company," Dad said. He was up on the ladder again, this time cleaning out the gutters.

"He didn't say anything about having company," I said, frowning.

"Maybe it's surprise company," Dad said. "You should probably stay away until his guest is gone."

My frown deepened. "But we were supposed to get Huey out tonight." I pulled a piece of paper out of my pocket and unfolded it. "I translated the 'Star-Spangled Banner' into Morse code. Took me forever."

I heard a sigh and the clap of the screen door closing behind me. Cassi, in her cheer clothes, had stepped out onto the porch. "Ick, make him stop talking like that, Daddy. Brielle is coming and if she hears him, she might die from his nerdiness."

"What was that?" I said loudly, my voice echoing down the street. "I couldn't hear you over the clinking of the medals you earned in space camp. Mom must be packing them. I hope she remembers to keep them with your space rover obstacle course completion certificate."

She glared at me, her fists planted on her hips in perfect cheerleader formation. "I don't know what you're talking about," she said. "You're the space nerd, not me."

"Are you sure?" I yelled. Brielle's mom's car turned the corner and crept toward us, the sun glinting off the windshield. "Because I definitely have a sister, named CASS-EE-OH-PEE-AH, who knows exactly who Phobos and Deimos are."

"Okay, shh, Arty . . . Daddy . . ."

"And that sister of mine, the one named CASSIOPEIA, looks a lot like you. Who are Phobos and Deimos again? I've forgotten. Huh. If only Cassiopeia were here to remind me . . ."

"Shut up, Armpit! Dad, make him stop."

"Oh! I know who Phobos and Deimos are! Pick me!" Dad said, raising his hand like we were in a classroom.

Brielle's car thumped into our driveway, and now we could make out Brielle's upturned I-just-smelled-the-inside-of-Tripp's-gym-shoe face. "If she'd remind me, I could stop talking about it. Phobos and Deimos, Phobos and Deimos . . . I wonder if Brielle might know." I snapped my fingers and made like I was going to follow Cassi off the porch and to the car.

Cassi turned abruptly and through a barely open mouth she hissed, "Fine. Mars's moons. Happy now?"

I grinned. "Yes! Thank you, Cassiiiiii." She started down the driveway. "But I'd be so much happier if I knew what Phobos and Deimos meant in Greek."

She shot a half-scared, half-furious look at me and loped down the driveway. Just as she opened the car door, I snapped my fingers and shouted, "Oh, yeah! Phobos and Deimos! Fear and Panic!"

She slammed the car door shut and they backed out of the driveway, and I would have felt really proud of myself for having given her such a hard time if my eyes had not immediately gone right back to the strange car in Cash's driveway.

"You think they'll leave soon?" I asked.

"Who?" Dad asked, then followed my gaze. "If you had plans, I'm sure his guest will be gone in time."

But they weren't. The sun began to set, and Tripp and I played catch in the front yard. The car was still there. The sun moved lower in the sky, and Mom made raisin spice cupcakes. Tripp and Priya and I ate them on the porch. The car remained. The sun lowered and Priya had to go practice her cello, and Tripp went home to babysit his baby brother Guts. The car was still there. I ducked inside to eat dinner. I thumbed through a *Discovery* magazine. I watched half an episode of a cartoon. I packed a snack and made a thermos of Kool-Aid and rolled up a blanket and stuffed everything into a back-pack. I loitered around the kitchen. I watched Mom pack the last of the knickknacks in our living room. And the car was still there.

Finally, I couldn't take it anymore. Just as I saw the first firefly blink, I went to Cash's door, hoping Dad wouldn't catch me and yell at me for not giving Cash and his company some privacy.

A woman opened the door. She had short gray hair and a smooth, friendly face and was holding a dish towel in one hand. There was a lamp on behind her in Cash's living room.

Wait. That should go in all caps.

THERE WAS A LAMP ON BEHIND HER IN CASH'S LIVING ROOM!

For a second, I feared I might have actually dreamed the whole thing and Cash Maddux didn't really live here. Which would have been both the best and worst dream ever.

"Hi," I said. "Is Cash home? Er . . . Mr. Maddux? Is he . . . here?"

She smiled down at me, one of those smiles my mom sometimes gives before she says something like, *Well, aren't you precious,* or *Bless your heart.* She shook her head. "I'm sorry. He's not."

"Oh. Okay," I said. "Can you tell him Arty came by?"

"Oh. You're Arty? The boy he's been stargazing with? He told me all about you." I nodded, and a little jolt of happy wound its way through me at the thought of Cash telling someone about me. But also a little jolt of disappointment at the word "stargazing." We weren't "stargazing," we were changing the course of humanity through scientific discovery!

"Please, come in." She stepped aside and let me through the door. Once I was inside, she shut the door, then sat on the edge of the couch and resumed her saintly smile. "I'm Cash's sister," she said. "You can call me Sarah."

"Okay," I said, still standing awkwardly in the doorway, afraid to sit on anything now that I'd seen it in full light. Cash's house was . . . ugly.

"Honey, I'm afraid Cash is in the hospital."

"What? Why?"

She looked at me sympathetically. "He isn't doing very well."

I felt myself go numb from the chin down. "How not very well is he doing?" I asked.

She shook her head sadly, tilted to the side. You know the news is never going to be very good when it's coming to you from a sideways head. "Did Cash ever tell you about his cancer?" she asked in a small voice.

And then I did sit down, but not by choice. My legs and butt pretty much made the decision for me, plopping me right down onto Cash's recliner. "He has cancer?" I asked.

"Lung cancer. He's had it for some time," she said. "And I'm afraid it's finally caught up with him."

I said nothing. What did that mean, *finally caught up with him*? She'd made it sound like a monster, rushing through the woods after him, leaping forward and snagging him by the ankles, making him fall into the leaves.

Immediately I thought about our last few walks back from Huey, how Cash had coughed and gasped and how he'd had to stop and put his hands on his knees a few times.

Maybe my vision of the cancer monster wasn't too far off.

"When will he get out?" I asked.

She did that sad head shake thing again, and I almost told her not to answer me at all, if her answer was going to begin with that shake or come out sideways. "I'm—I'm not sure . . ."

Suddenly it didn't matter that we were moving to Vegas. It didn't matter that the Bacteria ate all our food and talked only in single syllables. It didn't matter that the Brielle Brigade couldn't spell the word "science" or that I'd never climb into the tire rocket ship anymore or that I was walking around in a shoe that had once lived in Comet's stomach for a whole day.

All that mattered was that my friend was dying.

"Can I go see him?" I asked.

Sarah gazed at me for a long moment, squeezing the towel in her fist. *Open, close, open, close.* She stood and placed the towel on the couch where she'd just been sitting.

"Let's go ask your parents, and I'll get my car keys," she said.

29

A COMET'S TAIL (NOT THE DOG'S, BUT JUST AS SMELLY)

The hospital was white. White, white, white, everywhere I looked. White like the moon. White like the tail of a comet, the white of a meteor exploding under atmospheric pressure. Blindingly white.

Cash must have hated it there.

A nurse was standing by his bed, tapping something into a little electronic device that she slipped into her pocket when we came in. She squished an IV bag around and adjusted a blanket under his chin, smiling at us the whole time.

"He's been resting comfortably," she whispered to Sarah on her way out, and Sarah nodded gratefully.

I stood in the doorway, trying to take it all in. The beeping machines and the hiss of something squeezing and releasing. The tubes and the wires.

And the tiny, white-haired old man resting in the bed, his head smashed flat against the pillow, his eyes closed, his lips pale. One socked foot poked out from under the blanket, but otherwise, he was covered from chin to toe, like a mummy. Like somebody who was already dead.

He didn't even look like Cash. His skin was too thin, almost see-through, his breathing too labored and false, as if he were a machine man rather than a real human. I closed my eyes and tried to imagine the breathing sound to be inside the helmet in his space room instead.

The force is strong with this one (one-one).

I waited for my brain to take over, to hear mission control telling Cash and me it was time to take off, to hear us checking and ticking off the systems and buttons in our space shuttle one by one. I tried to imagine us floating around in the space station. Anything.

But nothing would come. All I could see was the whiteness of his skin. The brightness of that dying star of a hospital room.

"It's too bright in here," I said, and was surprised to hear my own voice sounding gruff, like Cash's. I walked over to the one window and yanked the curtains shut. Immediately the room dimmed. Better.

Cash's eyes opened at the *scrrr* sound of the curtains closing.

"Kid," he said. Groggy. Breathless.

I froze. "Hi," I said. I even gave a halfhearted wave, and then felt like a big dork about it.

"He came by. He wanted to see you," Sarah offered. She

took a few tentative steps toward her brother's bed but seemed half-afraid. "How are you feeling?"

He turned his head to look at her. A scowl creased his face. "How do you think I feel? Like running a marathon? I feel like I'm dying."

She took a step back and turned her face to the floor. I thought I saw a tear gather on the tip of her nose, but she kept her hands clasped together in the folds of her skirt.

Slowly, Cash snaked a hand out from under his blanket. He motioned for me to come closer. I did.

"Listen, kid," he started, but then for a long time he didn't say anything else and it felt really awkward, so I reached into my back pocket and pulled out the paper with the Morse code songs on it.

"I've got a new message to send," I said hopefully. "When you get out, we can send it up. I think we're getting close."

He shook his head impatiently. "Not gonna happen," he said.

"Sure it is," I said. "We've worked so hard, and I think Huey is really good—the best I've ever had, actually—and . . ."

He swiped at the paper in my hand. It tore on one edge and floated down to my feet. "I said it's not gonna happen," he said, his voice guttural and raspy, and began a coughing fit like none I'd ever heard out of him before. Now that I had a name for that coughing—*cancer*—it frightened me. "We're not gonna make contact with Mars," he finally said once he'd caught his breath again.

"I'll wait until you're better," I said weakly, and it wasn't until a tear gathered on the tip of my own nose that I realized I had been crying. "We'll do it together."

"Kid, listen to me," he said. "I've devoted my whole life to the sky. My whole life. It cost me marriage, kids, pets, everything. I had nothing but what was up there." He jabbed a weak finger toward the ceiling. "I spent every waking second studying what's up there. I used up everything I've got on what's up there. And you know what's up there?"

I shook my head, sniffed, did the hiccup-cry thing that babies and annoying little kids do.

"NOTHING!" he boomed, so loud both Sarah and I jumped and a nurse poked her head through the door curiously. He coughed for a moment, the end sounding weedy and agonizing, like words spilling out of his mouth rather than just air. "Nothing," he repeated more softly once he'd caught his breath and swallowed a few times. "There is nothing up there but rocks, and I wish more than anything that I'd given up on it when I still had time. I wish I'd paid more attention to life on Earth."

He turned his head so his watery eyes were gazing right into my watery eyes, and for a second I thought maybe I saw something in them that I recognized. Something I'd seen in Mom's eyes when she yelled at me to look both ways, or in Dad's eyes when he'd told us about Las Vegas. It was like a mixture of fear and protection. And maybe . . . worry?

"That project we've been working on? That contraption with the mirrors? It's all yours, kid," he continued. "But do us both a favor. Take it up to the hill and destroy it. Smash it to bits. It'll be just as useful destroyed as it is now. Destroy it and walk away and live your life."

I shook my head. "I can't . . ."

"You hear me, Arty?" Cash said. I bit my lip. This was the first time Cash had ever called me by my real name. "Give up on it while you still have a life. Stop wasting it on a pipe dream. You are never going to contact anyone on Mars or any other planet. You aren't going to prove that there's life out there. You aren't going to do anything that will make any difference as long as you're looking at life through a telescope. Give up. Before you turn into a pathetic, lonely old man dying alone on a plastic-covered mattress."

He coughed again, loud and long—so long I worried he might never stop.

"You're not alone," Sarah said softly. "We're here."

But I didn't want to be there anymore. I was crying like an idiot, and my insides felt hard and burned from his words. Give up? Just give up on everything I'd ever believed in? He was the first person who'd ever believed with me, the first person to ever understand why the sky was so important to me. And now he was telling me to just give up?

Worse, he was telling me to give up because . . . it was useless.

"Go," he said, and when Sarah and I didn't move, he barked it out again painfully. "Go! You're always hanging around where you're not wanted, kid! I didn't ask for you to come to my house. I didn't ask for you to break into my space room. I didn't ask for any of it."

Sarah and I locked eyes, with a *should we go?* type of look, and he coughed twice, winced like he was in great pain, and bellowed, "Get out of here, I said! Let an old man die in peace! Don't you have the sense to know when you're not wanted?"

My face burned with anger and confusion. It wasn't fair what he was doing. I came here because I . . . because I loved him. And he was smashing my dreams to bits. "You don't have any sense!" I yelled back, before my brain could catch up with my mouth. "You know that? You're the one with no sense! You have cancer and you keep smoking those nasty things and you don't even care that you're going to die and . . . and leave people behind!"

I bent to pick up the paper he'd knocked out of my hand. A whole night's worth of work, something I'd been so hopeful about just a few minutes before, now just felt like trash. I leaned over and dropped it into the wastebasket, then hurried to Sarah's side as she made for the door.

"Arty," Cash said. But I just kept walking.

30

HUEY AND THE GREAT SPACE EXPLOSION

Sarah didn't say much of anything as she drove me home from the hospital, other than that her brother wasn't himself right now and that she was sorry he'd said such awful things to me.

I wanted to tell her that, as far as I could tell, he was pretty much being exactly how he normally is, that he was so mean I originally thought he might murder me, and that I was used to him saying awful things to me. I wanted to tell her it wasn't her fault I was stupid enough to believe that Cash and I were friends. I wanted to tell her that it didn't matter anymore, because he was dying and I was moving, so what was the point of getting my feelings hurt? But instead I just stared out the window at the passing houses and wiped my snotty nose on the back of my hand and thought about what a dumb jerk I was for thinking Cash had been hanging out with me because he'd wanted to.

"Can I get my things? I left them in Cash's wheelbarrow,"

I said when we pulled into the driveway. Dad was still up on the ladder, flashlight in his mouth, pulling gunk out of the gutter by the old CICM-HQ. I glanced at him, thinking about how secluded and important I felt up there for all those nights. Like I could just reach up and touch the planet I was trying to contact. And there Dad was, pulling old leaves and Blow Pop wrappers out of the gutters just like it was any other part of any other house.

"Sure, honey," Sarah said as she fumbled around the visor until she located the garage door button. She pushed it and the door rumbled open. Right up front, there he was: Huey. Sitting in the wheelbarrow, just like always. Sarah walked up to it and poked around. "Is this the thing you two were working on together?" she asked. I nodded. "Maybe you should go ahead and take it, then. Just like Cash said. That way you can still work on it without him."

I gazed at Huey. If Cash hadn't gotten sick tonight, we would have been wheeling him up to the hill right about now. We would have been "Star-Spangled Banner"-ing the heck out of those Martians. And we would have been eating pastrami and pickles while we did it. "I'll be right back," I said.

I hurried across the yard. Our garage door was still open, since Dad was using the ladder. I went inside and found our wheelbarrow and wheeled it back to Cash's house. One by one, I took the parts and pieces of Huey out of Cash's wheelbarrow and put them in mine.

"Thank you," I told Sarah as I backed out of the garage.

"Are you going to be okay, Arty?" she asked. "Why don't you come inside? I'll make us a snack. We can talk if you like. I don't know much about space, but I know the stories my brother shared with me over the years."

"No, thank you," I said. "I'm fine. I'll be fine." I wasn't sure if that was true, but it felt like the right thing to say.

"Okay," Sarah said. She pushed a button to close the garage door. It hummed down steadily. "Well, if you change your mind, I'll be here. I plan to stay until . . . well, you know."

I guessed I did know. *Until the end,* is what she'd meant to say.

"Okay," I said, then maneuvered the wheelbarrow in a slow circle until I had it pointed the right direction. I stared at Huey, jiggling inside, clanking against himself, almost as if he were jittery and excited about tonight's adventure.

"Do us both a favor . . . destroy it . . . smash it to bits. . . ."

Tears collected in my eyes again as I thought about all our hard work putting Huey together. I'd been blind enough to think we were having fun, when to Cash all I was doing was invading his space—unwanted—and making him keep pursuing a dream he'd wanted to let die.

"Do us both a favor . . ."

Instead of heading straight over to our garage, I turned left and started through the backyard, my feet seeming to move without my willing them to. I pushed on straight for the woods.

Dad looked up when I passed him and turned the flashlight

on me. "Arty?" he asked. "What do you have there? Where are you going? Arty?"

He kept calling after me as I plunged into the woods, but I didn't answer him. I couldn't. I was too busy hearing Cash's horrible words in my mind, too busy seeing his papery grayish-white skin, too busy feeling his bellowing cough thunder through the room.

I practically ran down the path through the woods, not even worrying about bugs or bears or any of the other things I'd bothered Cash about that first night up the hill. All I could think of was getting to the top.

By the time I popped out into the clearing, I was sweating and crying and breathing really raggedly, like someone running from a monster in a horror movie. My whole body was shaking with rage and anger and fear and sadness and what felt like every emotion in the world rolled up into one. What I wouldn't have given to be the Bacteria at that moment, the only thought in my mind one syllable long, rather than the tangle of syllables tripping over each other. My head felt cluttered, full of stuffing.

I pushed Huey all the way to the zenith, where the moon shone down, and bent over with my hands on my knees, pulling in gaspy painful breaths.

"How could you?" I screamed, first to the ground, and then I looked up into the sky and repeated it, only louder, yelling at the moon. *"How could you?"* But I couldn't go any further, because the question was locked and loaded with so many endings:

How could you give up on Huey?

How could you give up on us?

How could you kill my dreams?

But worst of all, how could you die without telling me? Didn't I have a right to know? Isn't that what friends do—warn each other that the worst is about to happen?

Sarah was right. Cash had said a lot of awful things to me at the hospital. He'd said awful, unforgivable, unforgettable things. She probably thought the worst was telling me I was always hanging around where I didn't belong or something like that. But she was wrong. The meanest thing he'd said to me came at the very end: *"Give up on space."* Because he might as well have been telling me to give up on . . . us.

With a growl, I grabbed the handles of the wheelbarrow and pulled up with all my might. A disassembled Huey tumbled out onto the ground with a horrifying crunch. Or maybe it was a gratifying crunch. Somehow it was both at the same time.

Two of the mirrors broke on the initial fall. This was the beginning of the end. I raced toward the edge of the woods again. I searched around until I found a big stick, which I carried back to the heap of parts and started wailing on them. The spotlight cracked, the mirrors burst, the metal dented. I pounded and kicked and grunted and cried and said words that made no sense. I pummeled Huey with all my might, doing just as Cash had told me to do—destroying him, smashing him to bits. Smashing our friendship to bits.

"Arty!" I heard in the distance, but I kept going. "Arty!"

I heard again, only closer. Then I felt a pair of arms wrap around my waist and pick me up. "Arty, what's going on? What are you doing? What's wrong?" A torrent of questions into my twisting, contorted, angry face.

I opened my eyes to see that it was my dad holding me, and just like that I was totally spent. I dropped the stick and went limp, letting my face fall onto my dad's chest, not even caring that if anyone from Liberty Middle caught me being held by my dad while crying my eyes out it would mean a lifetime of torment and finding my underwear yanked up between my eyebrows on a daily basis.

"Arty, Arty, what's the matter?" Dad asked, lowering both of us to the ground next to the smashed bits of Huey.

"Let's just move," I bellowed into my dad's shirt. "Let's just finish packing and move."

31

THE UNEXPECTED SOLAR FLARE OF LOVE

For the next two weeks, we packed nonstop. Our closets were emptied, our cabinets bare. What was left was placed into suitcases to take on our long road trip to Nevada. I even helped this time, diligently wrapping things in brown paper and laying them out in boxes, taping the boxes shut and labeling them in magic marker:

KITCHEN
ARTY'S ROOM
VEGA'S BATHROOM: WARNING!
THIS BOX IS FULL OF SCARY GIRL STUFF!

A For Sale sign appeared in our front yard, and some guy in a pickup truck came and pulled Cassi's swing set out of our backyard and hauled it away. Comet stood at the front door and watched and I could swear I saw a doggy tear in his eye. A moving van pulled up to our curb and we spent a whole day filling it with furniture and boxes—everything that belonged to the Chambers family, stuffed into the sweltering inner corners of the giant metal rectangle of cargo space. I thought it was weird how everything in the lives of five people could be put into one van. How our lives seemed so much bigger before we had to move them away to somewhere else.

Well, not all our things were there.

Huey was still torn to smithereens on the hilltop. And as far as I was concerned, he was going to stay there forever. Or at least until the next person found him and harvested his scrap for something useful.

I tried not to think about Huey, because thinking about Huey made me think about Cash, which made me think about all kinds of terrible stuff, not the least of which was what might have happened to him over the two weeks since I'd visited him.

The van driver had arrived an hour before, and Mom was frantically stuffing "one last thing" in after another "one last thing." It was amazing how many "one last things" Mom had. Vega and the Bacteria huddled together on the porch, and Cassi locked herself in the bathroom, where I imagined her kissing the mirror good-bye.

I climbed up onto the eaves outside my window and looked out over the neighborhood for the last time. It was still amazing to me that the hill beyond the woods wasn't visible from old CICM-HQ, even when I was looking for it. I knew it was there, and a part of me wanted to see it, to say good-bye to it, but every time I thought about climbing down and going back there, Cash's voice flooded my head again.

"Let go of space."

"Hey," I heard from below, and there were Tripp and Priya, standing in my yard. Tripp awkwardly held a gift bag in one hand. Priya had a book tucked under her arm. I hadn't seen either one of them for a couple of days, mostly because I'd been hiding from them. Every time I thought of my two best friends, I was embarrassed by all the times I made them care about space for me—*"You're always hanging around where you're not wanted, kid"*—and of taking them up to the hill and making them act like Huey wasn't stupid. Plus, I was afraid if I tried to say good-bye, I might do something stupid like cry. Again. Something about moving turns a guy into a real fountain of joy, I tell you.

"Hey," I said.

"Can we come up?"

"Sure."

I waited a few minutes and then there they were, heads poking through the window at me. I scooted over to make room, and one by one they climbed out.

"Today's the day, huh?" Tripp said. I nodded. He paused. "It's gonna be weird going to school without you in the fall."

I nodded again. The fountain was threatening to spring to life once more.

Priya elbowed Tripp, and I saw a meaningful look pass between the two of them. And by "meaningful," I mean the kind of warning look Priya gives when she means to say shut your flapping gum trap before I sock you one, dummy. I'd seen that look more times than I could count.

She leaned forward. "My mom and your mom are already talking about spring break. I think we're going to come see you. My mom is going to talk to Tripp's mom about taking him with us."

Spring break was a long time away. Months away. Priya would probably have different bracelets by then. Or maybe even no bracelets at all. Tripp would probably . . . still be Tripp. Guys like Tripp never changed much.

"Cool," I managed.

Tripp shifted and handed the gift bag to me. "Here," he said. I looked at the tag.

TO: Arty
From: Trevor

Aha! Trevor was his real name! I . . . never would have guessed it, actually. Tripp totally didn't seem like a Trevor to me. Just a Tripp.

I pulled out the tissue paper. Inside the bag were Chase's old Mickey Mouse binoculars, which I'd given back to him the day Mom and I packed my room. The sight of them made my breath nearly catch in my throat. "I heard about what happened with Huey," Tripp said. "Chase said you could keep these instead. Well, he said it after I threw sock balls at his face for half an hour, anyway." Priya elbowed him and they shot looks at each other again. "Anyway, I thought maybe you could start over once you got out there."

"Thanks," I said, and decided not to tell him that I had no intention of starting over at all.

He shifted uncomfortably. "Also, I have something to tell you guys." Priya and I exchanged glances. She shrugged. "When Chase said I was at practice, he was telling the truth. I . . ." He trailed off, licked his lips, took a deep breath, let it out in a gust. "I've been taking ballet lessons."

"Ballet lessons?" Priya and I said at the same time. In a million years I would never have guessed ballet lessons. Drum lessons, chess lessons, yo-yo lessons, rodeo clown lessons maybe, but *ballet* lessons?

He blushed. "It's just . . . my mom thought it might help my clumsiness. A lot of football players take ballet, you know, so it's not as girly as it sounds. I actually really like it."

Priya and I nodded our heads appreciatively, but Priya mouthed the words *"ballet lessons"* to me and I shrugged.

"And, hey, it's working!" Tripp said. "That weekend that you couldn't find me? When you had to stay at Cash's house? I got third place at a competition in Columbia that day. They said my *relevé* was really sophisticated."

"Wow, good job, Tripp, that's great," Priya said.

"Yeah, man, that's really cool," I added.

He shrugged. "Anyway, I just thought you guys should know. I didn't like keeping secrets from you. Maybe sometime you can come see me at a recital or something. I think I might be a dancer when I grow up."

"Of course," I said. "Definitely."

"I almost forgot." Priya leaned forward and handed me the book. "I thought this might come in handy on your trip," she said. It was a road atlas. She reached across Tripp and flipped the pages until they were open to Missouri. She pointed to a red star that had been hand-inked right above the Missouri River near Kansas City. "I marked this so you wouldn't ever forget where we are."

As if I ever could.

"Thanks," I managed again, while on the inside the fountain raged and burst around so hard I felt I was floating.

We sat there for a few more minutes, Tripp asking all kinds of questions about my new house, which I'd only seen in pictures online. And then when I'd shrugged and grunted my way through those, he started in on more general questions: "Does your house have a Jacuzzi in the bathroom? Is it close to the Vegas Strip? Do they have yards in Vegas, or is it just desert sand? Do you have a slot machine in your bedroom? Do you have to wear a suit to go into a casino, like they do in the movies? Do you know how to play blackjack? How much money do you think you could win in one of those casinos, anyway? Do you think you'll end up being a magician, and, if so, would you have tigers? White one or regular ones? Or would you go for something totally different, like bears? Or penguins? Are there any magicians with penguins? That would be really cool, being a magician with penguins, don't you think?"

It was almost torture, because it was totally like Tripp to be asking questions like those. And it was almost torture, because sometimes Tripp's questions basically were torture. But that was what I was going to miss about him.

Priya must have been feeling kind of tortured, too, because after a while, she said, "Well, we should probably go so you can get ready to leave."

I was never going to be ready to leave, but I nodded anyway, and said, "Yeah," and next thing I knew they were scooting back in through the window. Tripp went in first—gracefully!—and Priya and I both craned for the window at the same time, our faces ending up just inches apart.

We stopped, grinned at each other, and then quick as lightning, she reached over and planted a kiss right on my cheek.

"See you in April, Arty," she said, and before I could even get feeling back into my stunned, buzzy face, she climbed through the window and was gone.

Whoa.

. . . Whoa.

I mean—did you—whoa—did you see that?

I stayed on the eaves for a long time, my fingers pressed to my cheek, the atlas and binoculars tucked in my lap, my two best friends chatting as they walked down the sidewalk just out of my sight. I scooted to the very edge of the eaves and peered around the corner to see if I could still see them.

And that was when I saw Sarah's car pulling into Cash's driveway.

32

CASHIUS KIDDIUS: THE FRIENDSHIP CONSTELLATION

I scurried back in through the window, closed it, and tossed the gifts my friends gave me into the open suitcase on my bed. As I rushed down the stairs, I passed Mom, who was coming up the stairs with one finger held up.

"I've just got to get one more thing and then we'll be ready to go," she said.

"Hey, what's the hurry, bud?" Dad asked as I raced past him down the porch steps. Vega and the Bacteria had moved to the Bacteria's car. I could see through the windshield that Vega was a mess. She had her head leaned into his shoulder, sobbing, while he took bites off the end of a roll of cookie dough just above her hair. Every so often he patted her head. "Don't go far," Dad yelled after me. "We're leaving soon! Your mom just has to get one more thing!"

I ran through our yards and caught Sarah just as she was opening Cash's front door. She had her purse looped over one arm and was juggling a bunch of mail.

"Oh," she said, startled, when I approached her. "Arty. So good to see you. How are you feeling?"

"How's Cash?" I asked, out of breath.

She shook her head sadly, sideways again. "Not good, I'm afraid."

"Can I go see him? I want to say good-bye. My parents will wait if I ask them to." I wasn't sure if this was true or not, but I was prepared to ask them. I hadn't realized it until that moment, but leaving without saying good-bye to Cash would have been like leaving without saying good-bye to Tripp and Priya. No matter how mean he was.

Somehow Cash managed to look even whiter than the last time I saw him. He was hooked up to machines everywhere, and there was so much blipping and beeping, I wondered how he could possibly sleep through it.

"He's just sleeping, right?" I asked nervously.

Sarah nodded. "I think so."

"Maybe we should go. He probably doesn't want me to wake him up." (Translation: I'm a big wimpy Orion and I'm scared and want to run away.) "Yeah, we should go."

But Cash must have heard us, because he opened his eyes. They were tiny slits over bloodshot and yellowing eyeballs, but they were open.

"Kid," he croaked, barely more than a whisper.

"I'm sorry, Cash," I blurted out. "I'm so sorry. I didn't mean to say the things I did. You have sense, you really do. I'm the one with no sense. And I did what you told me to do.

I destroyed Huey and I gave up on space. I'm moving today but before I go, I just wanted to tell you that I'm really, really sorry. For everything."

His forehead creased and he fumbled with one hand until he freed it from the blankets. He waved me over, looking impatient. My feet must have obeyed, because all of a sudden I was right next to his bedside. He waved more, so I leaned over. Closer. Closer.

He fumbled until his other hand surfaced. In it was a piece of paper. Weakly, he held it out to me. I took it. It was the paper I'd thrown in the trash last time I'd been here. The one with the Morse code "Star-Spangled Banner." He'd gotten it out of the trash.

He waved for me to inch even closer.

"Lovely cannons," he whispered into my ear.

"What?" I asked.

But he was beset with a coughing fit that cracked through the air like gunfire. It seemed to go on forever. A machine started beeping and a nurse came in and elbowed me away. She pushed some medicine into Cash's IV. Slowly, his cough stopped, and his eyes drooped closed again.

"Come on, Arty, I promised your mom we wouldn't be long," Sarah said softly. "He'll be sleeping for a while."

I followed, wondering what the heck "lovely cannons" meant.

When we got back to the house, Sarah patted my shoulder. "I know he didn't say much, but I'm sure he heard everything you said. He is really fond of you, Arty. And I know he's sorry, too."

"Thanks," I said.

"I'm glad you came by. I was hoping to catch you before you left. Cash gave me something to give to you. I'll be right back."

She disappeared inside the house. When she came back, she was holding a brown paper sack with handles, the kind you get from the specialty grocery stores. It smelled like cigar smoke. The scent made me miss Cash all the more. She handed the bag to me through the door. "He said to tell you that you will be okay in Vegas."

"Thanks," I said again, and started to leave, but turned back. "Do you know anything about lovely cannons?"

Sarah looked confused. "Lovely cannons?"

"Yeah, that's what he whispered to me. 'Lovely cannons.' I don't know what it means."

She shrugged. "I have no idea. Have you two discussed wars or something?"

We had. But only imaginary space wars. We'd never brought up cannons, because, duh, without gravity, what good would a cannon do? Clearly, a death ray was the only way to go for maximum destruction. "No."

"I'm sure it'll come to you."

"Yeah, maybe," I said. I gripped the bag tighter and stepped off the porch. "Thanks for everything," I said. "Sorry I won't be at the funeral."

"I understand," she said. "And so would Cash." I started

walking toward home and she leaned out the door. "And thank you, Arty, for being such a good friend to my brother. Probably the best friend he's had in a long time."

Back home, I took the bag up to my bedroom and shut the door. "Oh! Just one more thing!" I heard my mom chirp from somewhere within the house.

I sat on my bed and opened the bag at my feet. Inside was the astronaut helmet I'd worn when I'd visited Cash's house. Under the helmet was a letter. I placed the helmet on my head, the echoing of my own breath sounding familiar and wonderful. Carefully, I opened the letter, which was almost illegible in its shaky hand.

Dear Arcturus,

In the world of stargazing, the stars are labeled according to the Greek alphabet: alpha, beta, and so forth. The brightest star in any constellation, then, is its alpha star. As it happens, Arcturus is the alpha star in the Boötes constellation—the star formation known as the Herdsman. The Greeks used to refer to this constellation as the Arctophylax, or the bear watcher.

There are many stories surrounding the Boötes constellation, giving it ties to everyone from Atlas and Zeus to Dionysus.

But it is the alpha star—Arcturus—that has real importance in the night sky. Some stories say Arcturus was placed in the sky to protect Callisto and Arcas from Hera's jealousy. Some call Arcturus "Haris-el-sema," which means "the keeper of heaven." Still others call him "Hokulea," which translates to the "Star of Joy."

But I call Arcturus "Arty," or sometimes, "kid," and that, in my heart, translates to "friend."

It is hard for an old, bitter man like me to experience joy. Ever since Herbert Snotpicker (did that just for you) stole my life away from me, I have had a hard time even seeing what joy was. For the longest time it existed only in the sky for me. And then the sky blackened and it didn't exist at all.

Until you came along. The morning that you trespassed into my space room, it was almost as if a curtain had been lifted. I could see myself in your excitement. I could see the sky again! I could see joy again. I could dream again.

I could do those things all because of you.

I'm sorry for the rotten things I said to

you, kid. I wish I could take them all back. The truth is, my fear has come back something fierce. It looks like I'm going to die having never gotten up there, having never fulfilled my dreams, and I'm afraid if that happens, it will mean I have wasted my whole life. And I'm afraid of letting you waste your whole life, too.

After you left, I had the nurse pull out the paper you'd brought with you to the hospital, and it was then that I realized that, through you, my dreams may still be realized. Even if I'm gone, when you discover life on other planets, it will be as if I'm discovering it right along with you. Because a dream can never be truly realized until it's shared.

Huey was our dream, kid, and even after I die, I want you to keep trying, keep dreaming, keep looking to the sky. Kid, you keep dreaming, and I'll promise you one thing. If there is life out there somewhere, I will send you a sign.

Never give up. Especially on space, but never give up on anything. Especially never give up on yourself, like I did.

Notice I said "*when* you discover life on

other planets," not "*if* you discover life on other planets," because all that bunk I told you about it not being out there was just that—bunk. Hooey. A load of space garbage. A floating flock of Herbert's snotballs. It's not all dead rocks out there. I know that to my core.

I'm going to miss you, kid. I really am. You gave me something I'd never thought I'd be able to have. You gave me something Herbert Snotsflicker (you're right—that is kinda fun!) could never take away from me.

Arcturus, the red giant, the third brightest star in the sky, is 110 times brighter than the sun.

And that's what you gave to me.

I am thankful.

Yours in space,

Cash Maddux

P.S. I think you'll like the change I had Sarah make to the suit.

P.S.S. You still ask too many questions, though.

I read the letter twice, my hands making the paper shake. The fountain had sprouted to life again, only this time it raged too hard against the insides of my eyelids to keep it in. Tears rolled off my chin and plopped onto the helmet. But they were good tears. I was going to miss Cash. But at least I knew he was going to miss me, too.

After the second time I read the letter, I refolded it and placed it on the floor beside me. Then I reached into the bag and pulled out Cash's flight suit, which had been folded into the bottom of the bag. I held it up by the shoulders. Sarah had stitched letters across the front of it:

HUEY

And underneath, in tidy cursive:

Hillside Undercover Exploration of Yetis

I blinked. That was a terrible acronym. First of all, it made it sound like I was looking for your average variety Earth yeti, the kind you find in rain forests and mountain caves and stuff. Which I wasn't. And second, I wasn't just looking for yetis. I was looking for *Martian* yetis, and I'm pretty sure if I found one, doing a hula on a beach and waving a Mars is #1 foam finger at me, the fact that it was a *Martian* would probably far outweigh the fact that it was a yeti, and nobody would call it a yeti at all. Not to mention, being a Martian yeti would probably mean that it would be different from an Earth yeti, and maybe it wouldn't even be called a yeti but would have a different name, like a . . . Vega. Plus, I could never put it on a T-shirt, because everyone who saw me walking around with the word HUEY across my chest would naturally assume my name was Huey. Besides, was the plural of "yeti" even "yetis," or was it just "yeti"? Because "yetis" looked weird, and I did not want to have to get into some big grammar talk every time I wore my shirt.

On the other hand. Cash came up with an acronym. Cash said yetis. Which meant he had been listening to me. At least at some point, he had been paying attention to my hopes and dreams. Which made the acronym kind of . . .

"Perfect," I said aloud.

Just then, Vega and Cassi came into my room, their eyes red and swollen from tears to match mine.

"The van just left," Vega said softly. "It's time to go."

"What's that?" Cassi asked, and instinctively I let the flight suit drop back into the bag.

"Nothing," I said. I pulled off the helmet and put it next to the letter on the floor. "You'd think it's nerdy."

She bent over the bag and peered inside, then pulled out the suit and dangled it in front of her. Her eyes got big. "Is this a real flight suit?"

I nodded. "It was Cash's."

Vega joined Cassi, running her fingers along the American flag patch. "So cool."

Cassi dropped it back into the bag. "Is it true that he's dying?" she asked, kneeling next to me.

"Yeah," I said.

"That's a bummer," Vega said, sitting on the other side of me. "I'm really sorry, Arty. I know you guys were friends."

Cassi sniffled. "I'm really going to miss my friends," and when she said it, I kind of felt sorry for her, even though the Brielle Brigade were super annoying and they made Cassi hate space. It was hard to lose friends, even annoying ones.

"I'm going to miss Mitchell," Vega added, her voice brittle.

We sat in silence together. Then Vega said, "But we have each other, so that's a good thing. Can you imagine having to move away from all your friends if you didn't have old Armpit here to torment, Cassi?"

"Definitely not," Cassi said, wiping her cheeks and pushing my head toward Vega. Vega pushed it back toward Cassi and we all chuckled.

"I'm really sorry about cheerleading," I said to Cassi. "And face sucking," I said to Vega. "Your hand must feel really cold without the Bac . . . Mitchell attached to it."

"Thanks," they both said, and they got up to leave.

I walked over to my suitcase, dragging the paper sack with me. Somehow I was going to have to fit this stuff into my already-crammed suitcases.

"Hey, Arty?" Cassi said from the doorway. I turned. "I still think space is maybe the tiniest bit cool," she said. "But don't tell anyone, okay?"

I grinned. "Who would I tell?"

The hustling and rustling downstairs told me that it was

almost time to go. I unfolded Cash's letter one last time and read it over again.

Never give up. Especially on space.
Never give up on yourself.
Huey was our dream.

I pressed the suit and letter into my suitcase and hurriedly zipped it shut, then rested the helmet on top of it. Then I got to my feet and sprinted out of my room and down the stairs.

"Hey-hey-hey," Mom shouted. "Where are you going? It's time to get on the road."

"Just one more thing!" I shouted over my shoulder, and ran out the front door.

33

THE GRAVITATIONAL PULL OF THE MOTHER, ER...FATHER PLANET

Dad was on the hill when I got there. He was wearing a pair of gardening gloves and was bent over beside a big moving box.

"Dad? What are you doing here?"

He popped up and smiled when he saw me. "Hey, Arty! I'm just doing some last-minute packing." He placed a mostly intact mirror into the box. "Your mom send you to find me?"

He was so casual about what he was doing, like this was something he did every day. Like this was no big deal. Like it was totally expected. Like he couldn't imagine leaving Huey behind, either.

I loved my dad. I mean, I loved my dad every day, but that was he's-my-dad-so-I-love-him kind of love. Watching him bend over and sift tiny nuts and bolts out of the grass, I realized that today he deserved he's-a-pretty-cool-person-so-I-love-him kind of love.

I never answered his question, so he pulled off his gloves

and came over to me. He put his arm around me and we both sat on the ground.

"Guess your life's pretty horrible right now, huh?" he said.

I nodded. "I don't even know what the pizza is like in Nevada."

"I'm sure it's pretty similar to the pizza in Liberty. You'll like it there, Arty. It's not that different."

"Yes, it is," I said. "Priya and Tripp won't be there. And neither will Cash."

Dad's arm hugged tight around me. "I know. And I'm sorry about that, pal. I really am. But I need you to roll with this. I need you to at least try to like Las Vegas. Your opinion matters to me."

I looked up at him. "Really?"

"Of course it does. You're the only one in this family who loves space as much as I do. You built this awesome machine." He swept his arm out to indicate what was left of the pieces in the grass. "You're a smart guy, Arty. Maybe even a genius. Moving, starting a new job, it's scary for me, too. I could use a genius on my side."

I smiled. It never occurred to me that this move wasn't just happening to Vega, Cassi, and me. It was happening to Mom and Dad, too. "Cash is going to die, Dad."

"I know. I'm really sorry, son. You two seemed close."

"He liked space as much as you do, too. It was kind of his whole life. That's why I can't leave Huey here."

Dad's forehead crinkled. "Who's Huey? Oh. The machine.

Gotcha." He stood up with a grunt. "Well, what do you say we box the rest of Huey up, then?"

I took his hand and let him pull me up, but before we got started, he spread his arms out wide and I plunged into them for a hug. "It's all gonna work out, Arty, you'll see," he said into the top of my head.

We started back toward the box, and Dad stopped. "Oh! I almost forgot!" He fumbled in his front pocket, pulled out a cell phone, and handed it to me. "I figured you would want a way to keep up with your friends on the way out to Nevada."

I turned it over in my hands. "Is it new?"

He bent, picked up a piece of Huey, and tossed it into the box. "Yep. And it's all yours."

I pushed a few buttons. He had already programmed Tripp's and Priya's numbers into the contacts, along with his, Mom's, and the Las Vegas Planetarium and Observatory. And . . . Sarah's? I turned the phone off and just watched my dad for a moment, smiling. I'd been so mad at him about moving for so long, I forgot what a really good guy he could be.

He stood to put a piece of Huey in the box and caught my eye. "And if Cassi gives you any trouble about that phone, you just send her to me."

Correction: a really *great* guy.

34

THE SPACE SHUTTLE EPIPHANY, READY FOR LIFTOFF!

In case you were wondering, it is 1,365.84 miles from Liberty, Missouri, to Las Vegas, Nevada. That's twenty hours of driving. Or, in my case, twenty hours of sitting between the two most annoying sisters on Earth and wishing a UFO tractor beam would suck me right through the roof of the car.

When they weren't busy whining about the radio station, they were fighting over earbuds. They complained that it was too hot, and then when Mom put on the air conditioner, they griped that they were freezing. Cassi practiced her cheers for 947 hours straight, and Vega's phone beeped with text messages more often than I blinked. They both bellowed that my legs were touching theirs and that my breath smelled like something died in my mouth and that my atlas was getting in their way.

Comet sat in the row of seats behind us and, every ten seconds or so, licked the back of my head. My hair was plastered to my scalp with dog drool. Which made Cassi and Vega complain even more.

Behind Comet were our suitcases and a box filled with clanking broken pieces of Huey.

I passed the time by memorizing the years that Halley's Comet passed through our solar system, going all the way back to 1066, and trying to imagine what it would look like from the top of Olympus Mons, the sixteen-mile-high volcano on Mars.

I also passed time by flipping the pages of the atlas Priya gave me, keeping track of the towns we passed.

That was what I'd been doing when I saw it.

After an eternity, we'd finally crossed over into Nevada and I was able to flip to the final page of our journey. The brush and dirt, and even the hazy mountains off in the distance, had gotten boring, so I followed I-15 with my finger, tracing how far we had left to go. We were just outside of Moapa; not far now. My eyes wandered past Vegas and up the page a bit, and my finger stopped.

"Lovell Canyon," I whispered. Excitement jolted through me. "Lovell Canyon! Lovely cannons!" I shouted, and Cassi, who'd been dozing, jerked awake.

"Ready! Okay! We've got spirit yes we d . . . ," she muttered before falling back to sleep.

I ignored her. "That's it! That's what Cash meant!"

Mom twisted around in her seat to see what was going on. "What's the problem?" she asked.

I pointed to the atlas, turning it so Mom could see it. "Not lovely cannons! Lovell Canyon! It's a place outside of Las Vegas."

Mom squinted at the map. "What about it?"

"Don't you see? He wasn't talking about some sort of war. I knew it!"

"Who?" Mom asked, looking thoroughly confused at this point.

"Cash! He was telling me where to take Huey!"

35

3-2-1 CONTACT!

Mars was in opposition in April the next year. Which gave me eight months to prepare. I spent most of those months saving up my money to buy new parts to replace the unfixable ones on Huey. But I also spent lots of time sprucing up the broken parts, including painting him navy blue, with stars and planets, really making him look the part. After all, if Huey and I were going to discover life on another planet someday, we had to be camera ready for when the press came after us.

I also painted across one side:

In Memory of CASH:
Contacting Aliens in the Solar System through Huey

Technically, that would be CASSH. Or CAITSSTH.

. . . Yeah, I was never going to get any good at acronyms.

It turned out my house in Las Vegas was kind of cool. It had a red tile roof and a stone wall around the yard. It was way bigger than our old house and had a pool right down the street. But mostly it just seemed like a house in a neighborhood, just like in Liberty. It made me feel like I hadn't really moved all that far away and that people were basically the same no matter where you went.

And the best part? Right outside my bedroom window was a little slope of roof, one just the perfect size for stargazing. Or for changing the course of human history through scientific discovery. However you want to look at it.

I liked my new school and right away made two new friends. Their names were Toby and Tan, and they both lived right down the street from me. We met on the first day of school, on the bus, and it turned out we all had PE and lunch together. Toby was into video games and Tan constantly had his nose smudged up against the pages of a book. Neither of them was interested at all in space, and neither of them fell a lot or wore clanky bracelets, but that didn't really matter. I liked them anyway.

Dad, however, did get interested in space again. Turned out that working for the new company meant he spent a lot less nighttime hours at work. Instead, he came home and we'd climb out onto the red tiles together, sitting side by side, sharing popcorn or chips or sometimes pastrami sandwiches in Cash's honor. Dad bought two pairs of binoculars—one for each of us. They weren't quite as cool as Cash's but somehow that seemed right. And I would tell him about the things I learned from Cash.

"Hey, Dad, have you ever heard of Gliese five eighty-one?"

"Nope."

"It's a star, and it's got this huge exoplanet, and there was a radio signal and this professor says …"

Mom and Priya's mom video called each other on the computer every day. And Mom stopped baking raisiny things.

Vega found a new boyfriend right away. His name was Vincent, and he was skinny and wore really tight black jeans with big, clomping boots. His favorite word was "yo" and he liked to use it in pretty much every sentence, like, "What's up, Arty, yo? School was a beast today, yo. Tomorrow's the weekend, yo." Vega was head over heels in love with the guy (yo), but I liked to think of him as the Virus (yo), and secretly he made me miss Mitchell a little bit.

Cassi found a new cheer squad, and it seemed like every girl on it was named Adrian. But Cassi's best friend Adrian thought I was cute and giggled a lot when I was around, and said it was "neato" how "like, smart and stuff" I was about "you know, those, like, space thingamabobby things." She drove me crazy when she was around, but at least Cassi started to hate space a little less, and sometimes she would even join Dad and me out on the rooftop, smacking her cinnamon gum and claiming every five seconds she saw a UFO.

"Did you guys see that?"

"It was an airplane."

"But it had lights and they were flashing!"

"Because it was an airplane."

"And it was moving across this way. Actually moving!"

"Because that's how airplanes get to the airport. Which is, by the way, the same direction the plane was moving."

"I'm telling you, it was a UFO."

"Next thing you know, Cassi, you'll be claiming zombies are real."

Aunt Sarin visited once, and brought baby Castor with her. He was googly-eyed and drooly, and he grabbed my finger and squeezed it just like Cassi used to do when she was a baby. Once, when Mom and Aunt Sarin were gabbing in the kitchen, I tiptoed into the living room with a gift for Castor.

"Hey, little star," I said, crouching so I was eye level with him in his baby swing. He smiled and cooed. "I have something for you." I held up Chase's old Mickey Mouse binoculars. Castor reached out with clumsy hands and grabbed at them. Once he got hold of them, he immediately stuck them in his mouth. "These binoculars are all yours. But they aren't just any binoculars. They're part of a very intricate piece of space-communication machinery. I expect you to take good care of them, okay? And when you're old enough, I'll show you an even better telescope." He gurgled and laughed. Chase's binoculars would be in good hands with Castor. Cash probably would have liked to see baby Castor gumming up those awful binoculars.

Speaking of Cash.

Sarah called a few days after we arrived in Vegas to tell me he had died.

"Don't you worry, I was right there with him all the way up until the end," she said.

I'd never had to talk about someone dying before and I wasn't sure what I was supposed to say. I tried to think of what Dad would say. "Did he, um, suffer?"

"No, he went very peacefully."

"Good, good," I said in my Dad-impersonation voice.

"The funeral was very nice, Arty. You should have seen it. Beautiful flowers, beautiful music. Your little friends both came. I can't remember their names. Red-haired boy, and a girl wearing lots of bracelets."

"Tripp and Priya?"

"Yes! That's it, Tripp and Priya. They said they didn't know Cash, but they knew you would want them there. They were such nice kids."

My chest felt warm. "Yeah, they're pretty cool," I said. "The best friends ever."

"Oh, and that reminds me. Some of Cash's old buddies from NASA were there. One came all the way up from Florida. I hadn't seen old Herb in years."

"Wait. Herbert Swanschbaum? He came?"

"Yes, and oh, did he have some stories to tell about Cash. Really fun ones. Herb was so broken up about Cash's death. He told me Cash was the best friend he ever had. Said he was so jealous of my brother."

"Herbert was jealous of Cash?"

"Sure was. Herb said most of the guys wanted to be an

astronaut for the status. They were out to be heroes. But Cash wanted to be an astronaut because he loved space and couldn't think of anywhere else he'd rather be. He didn't care about being anybody's hero. He was in it for the love."

I couldn't help but think that somehow Cash had ended up a little bit of a hero anyway. At least to one kid who just wanted to believe in life on Mars. I wished I had gotten the chance to tell him that, and I hoped that he knew it anyway.

That night, I told Cassi and Dad I wanted to look at the stars alone.

Fall came and went, and so did Halloween and Thanksgiving and Christmas. I missed Missouri snowstorms and sledding down Killer Hill with Aunt Sarin. But soon it was spring. Which meant spring break was coming, along with Tripp and Priya, but first it meant that Mars was in opposition and a shiny repainted Huey was up and ready to roll.

Dad and I packed sleeping bags and jackets, just in case it got cold. We took water bottles and sodas and Mom made us a tub of cookies. We rolled Huey into the back of the SUV and took off for Lovell Canyon, which was perfect for seeing the sky. Even better than up on the hill behind the woods.

It took us a long time to find a spot where it would be just the two of us, and then to park, unload, and set up Huey. But in some ways it was the best time of my life, laughing and sharing stories with Dad, the excitement of firing up new and improved Huey for the first time since Cash died. Now that Dad didn't work in an observatory anymore, he seemed to like space a lot better. He told me that was because his hobby and his job were two separate things again.

We rolled out our sleeping bags and hung our binoculars around our necks.

"You ready?" Dad asked as I poised over the on/off switch on the spotlight.

And suddenly I was nervous. Something about the air felt . . . charged somehow. Like something big could happen, and if I wasn't paying attention, I would miss it. I had never done this without Cash, and I wasn't sure what kind of feelings would come up when I pushed that button. I swallowed, licked my lips, nodded. "Yeah. I'm ready."

"Go for it," Dad said, turning and training his binoculars in the direction of Mars.

I reached down and flipped the switch.

Four dots. Another dot. Dot-dash-dot-dot, twice. Three dashes.

HELLO

I put my binoculars to my eyes and squinted around the bat butt until the black edges went away and all I was looking at was the distant red planet. Dad and I were still as statues, barely breathing.

And then Dad gasped. "Did you see that? Did you see, Arty?"

I held my breath, afraid to blink. I had seen it. A brief flash of light blinking over the planet. "Was that . . . ?" I started, but then it happened again. And again. And again. Dots and dashes.

....../../...../..-/./-.--

"What does that mean, do you think?" Dad asked, lowering his binoculars. I lowered mine as well, the fountain burbling happily beneath my eyelids again.

"It's Morse code," I said.

"What's it saying?"

I sat down heavily on the ground, my whole body welling up with so much possibility I felt like I could run a marathon and solve calculus puzzles and cook a turkey dinner all at the same time.

"Kid, you keep dreaming, and I'll promise you one thing. If there is life out there somewhere, I will send you a sign."

"You okay, Arty?" Dad asked. "You look funny. What did it say?"

"It said, 'HI HUEY.'" I turned my face up to the sky and smiled.

FUN FACTS ABOUT MARS

Hi, again! Arty here. Thought you got rid of me, didn't you? Wait—don't turn the page yet! I promise this won't take long. Since this story is called *Life on Mars*, I figured you should know a thing or two about the fourth planet from the sun so you don't get burned when asked about it.

* Mars was named after the Roman god of war because of its bloodred color. Which is kind of gross. And also wrong. It turns out Mars isn't red because of blood. It's red because of all the iron rusting in its soil.

* Mars's two moons, Phobos and Deimos, might actually be captured asteroids and look like potatoes. I think it would have been cool to name them Fries and Tots.

* Mars's version of the Grand Canyon is a huge canyon called Valles Marineris, which is about the length of the entire United States and is four miles deep. Yet I am convinced that Tripp wouldn't see it and would fall right in.

* Mars has polar caps just like Earth does. But don't start wondering whether those polar caps have penguins, because you'll get sidetracked drawing Martian penguins for about three hours. Trust me on this.

* During the winter, Mars gets so cold that almost a quarter of the atmosphere freezes. Sort of like

that time we were sledding and Tripp's sneeze froze to his face.

✳ Mars's atmosphere is very thin and made up of mostly carbon dioxide, so it would be impossible for humans to breathe there without a space suit. Sort of like trying to breathe in a blanket fort with Tripp when he goes all sleepover nebula on you.

✳ Scientists named some of the rocks on Mars's surface funny names like Scooby Doo, Barnacle Bill, Lumpy, and Hedgehog. There's even one named Eyebrow. Speaking as someone named after an armpit, I don't think Eyebrow's so bad.

SPACE ANIMALS

When I talked about Comet yipping at my heels inside a doggy space helmet, you probably thought I was crazy. I mean, don't you need thumbs and stuff to operate a flying object? Turns out, lots of animals have been in space. Here are a few:

✳ In 1948 and 1949 the United States sent several rhesus monkeys into space using a V-2 rocket. This was called the Albert series, because all the monkeys were named Albert. Basically, if someone tells you they're going to strap you to a rocket and launch you into space and you're the fourth Albert they've sent in a year, and come to think of it, you haven't seen any of the other

Alberts in a really long time . . . you might consider running away.

✳ Yorick, a monkey who took a 236,000-foot flight into space on an Aerobee missile in 1951, got the title of First Monkey to Survive a Trip to Space. He was mostly glad his name wasn't Albert.

✳ In 1957 the Soviet Union named a stray dog Laika, stuck her on Sputnik 2, and launched her into space. Laika's name meant "Husky" in Russian, but the United States nicknamed her "Muttnik." Laika made it into space just fine, but they forgot to figure out a reentry strategy, so Laika probably should have been named Albert.

✳ "Ham" sounds like the name of the first pig in space, but it actually stands for Holloman Aero Med (because astronauts aren't any better at coming up with acronyms than I am). Ham was the first chimpanzee to make a suborbital flight, and since Ham made it out okay, they decided maybe Alan B. Shepard Jr. would too. He was the first American to launch into space.

✳ Enos was the first chimp to hop into a Mercury Atlas rocket (okay, I don't know for sure that he hopped. In fact, I think it's pretty unlikely that he hopped. He may have skipped or climbed or been carried or even just plain walked in a chimpy way). He orbited the earth on November 29,

1961. Thanks to Enos's successful flight, John Glenn was able to orbit the earth just a few months later, in February 1962.

✳ You probably couldn't count how many mice have been launched into space, starting way back in 1948, when a couple of them tagged along with the Alberts. Also rats, guinea pigs, rabbits, and loads of fruit flies and other insects have been sent into space. In April 1998, the seven crew members of space shuttle *Columbia* were joined by over two thousand creatures. Now, that is one crowded spaceship! I wonder if any of them were named Albert.

CASH'S AND ARTY'S MORSE CODE TRANSMISSIONS

.-- . / -.-. --- -- . / .. -. / .--. . .- -.-. .

WE COME IN PEACE

- .- -.- . / -- ./ - ---/ -.-- --- ..- .-. / .-.. . .- -.. . .-.

TAKE ME TO YOUR LEADER

.... --- .-- .----. ... / - .... . / .-- . .- - .... . .-. / ..- .--. /

- .... . .-. . ..--..

HOW'S THE WEATHER UP THERE?

.-- .... . .-. . / .. ... / - .... . / -... .- - .... .-. --- --- -- ..--..

WHERE IS THE BATHROOM?

.. .----. .-.. .-.. / .... .- ...- . / - .... . /
... .--. .- --. .... . - - ..

I'LL HAVE THE SPAGHETTI

-.-. --- -- . - / . .- - ... / -.. .. .-. - -.-- / ... --- -.-. -.- ...

COMET EATS DIRTY SOCKS

...- . --. .- / ... -- . .-.. .-.. ... / .-.. .. -.- . / -.. .. .-. - -.-- /
... --- -.-. -.- ...

VEGA SMELLS LIKE DIRTY SOCKS

-.-. .- ... . / .. ... / .- / -.. .. .-. - -.-- / ... --- -.-. -.-

CASSI IS A DIRTY SOCK

ACKNOWLEDGMENTS

Many awesome people work hard to turn an idea into a book. I'd like to thank some of them now.

As always, first and foremost, I thank my agent, Cori Deyoe, for encouraging me to write a middle-grade story featuring a boy main character. Once again, you knew what I could do before I knew what I could do.

Really good editors are as precious as a foam finger–wearing Martian yeti with a flashlight and a working knowledge of Morse code. Thank you, Brett Wright, for the amazing and thoughtful revisions, the support, the enthusiasm, and especially the doodles. You are out of this world!

Special thanks to Michelle H. Nagler for being the first to love Arty's story, Nicole Gastonguay for the gorgeous design work, Linette Kim for giving Arty an early read, and Sandra Smith and Pat McHugh for double-checking my space facts and not throwing moon rocks at my head over all the punctuation errors.

I would have no story and no Arty if it weren't for the curiosity and comic relief of my longtime space buds and travel partners, Weston and Jane. Thank you also to the presenter at the Kansas Cosmosphere and Space Center planetarium in Hutchinson, KS, for making me giggle about an armpit, and to Camp KAOS for making space awesome.

Susan Vollenweider, my friend and first reader, thank you for reminding me that I have middle-grade boy character material surrounding me every second of the day. And for introducing me to sugar-free vanilla caramel coffee creamer, which, trust me, is a huge part of the construction of this book.

#1 in my life, in my heart, and in my corner—biggest, Jupiter-sized thanks are always reserved for Paige, Weston, Rand. You guys are the sun I revolve around. And, Scott, my galaxy can't even exist without you. I love you.